shackled

Also by Tom Leveen

Party

Zero

manicpixiedreamgirl

Sick

Random

shackled

TOM LEVEEN

SIMON PULSE
New York   London   Toronto   Sydney   New Delhi

SIMON PULSE

An imprint of Simon & Schuster Children's Publishing Division

1230 Avenue of the Americas, New York, New York 10020

First Simon Pulse paperback edition August 2016

Text copyright © 2015 by Tom Leveen

Cover photograph copyright © 2015 by Stephen Mulcahey/Arcangel Images

Also available in a Simon Pulse hardcover edition.

For information about special discounts for bulk purchases, please contact
Simon & Schuster Special Sales at 1-866-506-1949 or business@simonandschuster.com.

The Simon & Schuster Speakers Bureau can bring authors to your live event. For more information or to book an event contact the Simon & Schuster Speakers Bureau at 1-866-248-3049 or visit our website at www.simonspeakers.com.

Book designed by Regina Flath

The text of this book was set in Minion Pro.

Manufactured in the United States of America

2 4 6 8 10 9 7 5 3

The Library of Congress has cataloged the hardcover edition as follows:

Leveen, Tom.

Shackled / Tom Leveen. — First Simon Pulse edition.

p. cm.

Summary: When Pelly sees her best friend, who disappeared six years ago, in a coffee shop with a strange man, she's determined to discover the truth of her friend's disappearance and rescue her from her current captor.

[1. Kidnapping—Fiction. 2. Best friends—Fiction. 3. Friendship—Fiction. 4. Dating (Social customs)—Fiction. 5. Emotional problems—Fiction. 6. Mystery and detective stories.] I. Title.

PZ7.L57235Sh 2015

[Fic]—dc23

2014022800

ISBN 978-1-4814-2249-9 (hc)

ISBN 978-1-4814-2250-5 (pbk)

ISBN 978-1-4814-2251-2 (eBook)

shackled

ONE

Like a heart attack. That's the best way to describe it. I've never had one of those, that I know of, but I'm pretty sure it feels just like that. Dr. Carpenter even agreed with my description. But I hadn't seen her in a few months.

Maybe that was a mistake.

"You're late, Pelly," David said to me as soon as I walked in the door of the Hole in the Wall Café.

I didn't answer. Couldn't. When the attacks come, I can't really speak. Or if I can, all that comes out is muttering, stuttering stupidity.

The Hole was a safe zone for me. A place I could trust. It took a while to attain that lofty status. And there aren't many such places. But I couldn't stay inside. I dumped my bag behind the counter before pivoting right back around and rushing outside, panting.

It helped that the sun was out. Nighttime tended to be worse, although I didn't know why. I guess because it's harder to see. I pulled a soft pack of Camel Lights and a cheap blue disposable lighter out of my hip pocket and lit up. Most people start when they're twelve or thirteen. I waited till last year. Because I'm that dumb.

I paced along the sidewalk in front of the Hole, taking long, purposeful strides. Like a soldier on guard duty. Stop, pivot, walk back the way I came. Deep drag, hold, blow out. Stop, pivot, repeat.

It's almost like OCD at this point. Everything has to be *just so*. If I can keep walking and be outside, the panic will pass. Usually. Eventually.

After a few minutes David poked his head out the front entrance. "Pel?" he said as I stalked past.

I blew out a harsh breath of smoke. Kept walking. My heart wasn't beating fast anymore. Instead it beat hard, and that was almost worse. Like my heart wasn't pumping so much as knocking from the inside, *bam! bam! bam!* Let me *out!*

"You okay?" David said as I walked past in the other direction.

My free hand clenched and unclenched of its own accord. The muttering and stuttering began.

"It was a guy, this *guy*, he was staring, he was just *staring*, this *guy* . . ."

I watched the gray concrete beneath my feet as I chanted. A little voice whispered to me that David had never seen me like this. I'd never wanted him to. I never wanted *anyone* to. Reason number 3,854 I didn't go to a real school anymore. I'd meant working here to be the first step toward going to school again someday, but—

"Someone hassled you on the bus?" David asked, stepping out into the sunlight. He jerked his head to one side to get his long, splintery bangs out of his eyes.

I almost snarled a laugh at him. The bus? Right. One isolated girl among crowds of people I didn't know, in a vehicle I could not control? Not happening. I walked everywhere—which wasn't many places—or got rides from Mom. I should've had a license by now, and instead I got carted around like a pathetic loser.

"Seven-Eleven," I said to David, and stopped walking. Stayed a few feet away from him. I hadn't gotten control of my breathing yet. The exercise and adrenaline and nicotine were making me nauseated. I'd all but run here from the store. "I was buying a pack and there was this guy, he just kept staring, and I thought . . . I mean, he just . . ."

I took a drag. Blew it out. Took another. Held it.

"So, are you okay?" David asked again. Like he didn't know what else to say.

I took my last puff and pitched the butt into the dirt parking lot.

"Doesn't matter," I said. "Forget it."

"Okay, well, *that* was bitchy, in case you were wondering."

"I dunno, I dunno, okay, I just, he was *looking* and he wouldn't stop *looking* and I can't *deal* with that . . ."

David took one step toward me. Slow. Like I might cut him. My fingers dug into the coin pocket of my jeans, made sure my pillbox was there. I knew it was. Never used the blade inside it while at work. But maybe today. I wondered if David knew about it somehow.

"Did he say anything?" David asked. "Did he do something to you? You want me to call the cops?"

Cops.

The word acted like a switch thrown at the base of my neck. My hands froze into fists. I stared into David's hazel eyes, which he shaded from the early afternoon sun while he looked at me.

"No." My breath shuddered as I sucked in fresh air. "No. He didn't. Nothing happened. He just, he freaked me out. Is all. I'll be okay."

"Nothing for nothing, but you don't look okay."

I tried to ease my panting down to a slower rhythm. Force more air into my lungs.

"What's that even mean?" I said.

"What, 'nothing for nothing'? I don't know. It's probably just a corruption of 'not for nothing,' but come to think of it, I don't know what that means either."

"Splendid," I said.

David looked like he didn't know whether to laugh or be pissed. I didn't know which I wanted him to be. *God,* my brains were like scrambled eggs.

"Just need a minute," I said before he could respond. My

knees shook, urging me to keep walking. Walk off the fear. Walk off the panic.

"I'm not punching you in," David warned.

"Fine."

David kept his eyes on me for another second. "But I guess I could cover for you. We're not exactly slammed."

"Yeah, sure," I said, and began pacing again. I couldn't stop myself. I could pace, or I could scream. One or the other.

"Or 'Thank you, David' is another option," he said, and went back inside the café.

"Thank—" I started, but the door closed.

Again: splendid.

And David is the coworker who is nicest to me.

I rested my hands on my hips as I paced again. My heart finally eased up, stopped throwing its elbows against my rib cage. I wanted another cigarette but forced myself not to. Maybe I hadn't been doing it long enough to really be addicted. I hoped so. I wanted to stop. But nicotine was my only medication. At least I could think when I smoked.

Maybe I shouldn't have flushed my pills. I couldn't get another scrip without Dr. Carpenter's permission. Five years with her—you'd think she'd make it so I could get a refill or two without her, but no.

I went ahead and smoked another cigarette but snuffed it out halfway. By then I felt like I could go inside. Not a single customer had come and parked in the dirt lot during that time.

I found David reading a book at the service counter as the

door closed behind me. That's how not-busy we were on a Wednesday afternoon.

David let his paperback book whisk to a close. The cover read *Tai Chi Classics*.

"That seemed pretty epic out there," he said. He narrowed his eyes cautiously, trying to figure where my mood was. I knew the look. He did it several times per shift. God. I belong back in the hospital. Or a zoo.

I came around the counter, passed him, and grabbed my blue apron from a peg on the wall. "Don't worry about it."

"Well, it's just—"

I held up my hands. "Just don't, okay? Please? Please."

David raised his hands back at me. "Fine, okay," he said. "Sorry." He turned to his book.

I started pulling at the brown rubber band on my left wrist. Snapped it against my skin. Once, twice, three. Once, twice, three. *Stop intrusive thoughts,* chanted Dr. Carpenter in my head. *Stop intrusive thoughts.*

By finishing the tying of my apron, I'd officially completed every job there was for me to do at that moment. I crossed my arms and leaned against the side wall, watching David read. If he noticed I was watching, it didn't bother him.

"I texted you to give you a heads-up that you were running late, in case you forgot or something," David said. Maybe he'd sensed me watching him after all.

"You did?" I pulled my phone out. The screen stared back blankly, like a shark's eye.

"I forgot to charge it," I said. That was stupid. So stupid. What if there was an emergency?

"You forgot to charge it—*again*," David corrected, and smiled.

I swear I tried to smile back, I really did. I guess I needed to learn how to do that. Smile, I mean. I know I'm not a bowl full of sunshine. When I smile, I'm afraid I look like I've got gas cramps or something.

I think somewhere in here is a real smile, hidden behind too many zits and hair that needs cutting or at least styling. My last haircut was a year ago. I'm one-less-shampoo a week from dreads. I hope people think it's this tangled on purpose.

"Yes, again," I agreed. No smile.

David made as if to smack my shoulder. I sidestepped out of the way. There followed that awful, awkward moment where he knew I had dodged and he ended up looking dumb. I hate that I do that. It happens at home, too. With hugs or incidental contact.

"Sorry," I said quickly.

David shook his head and made some kind of noise that was probably three or four phrases all jumbled together.

"Has it been busy?" I asked, to get us moving in another direction. *Any* direction.

"Not really," David said. "I hope you didn't rush."

"Not exactly."

"Good," he said. "So how do you buy cigarettes? You're not eighteen."

"I got a guy."

I didn't want to give away anything more. Like, it wasn't a guy. Alecia, nineteen and ultra bipolar, bought me up every week. Three packs. We met last year, which is when I started smoking. Maybe she had access to some pam, too, that I could bum or buy off her. That's what she called her Klonopin prescription, "pam." Maybe that's what all the cool kids called it. I wasn't one of those, how could I know?

No. I didn't need—I didn't want any meds. I could stop. I *had* stopped. I had everything I needed to get over this. I could get better without them. Without anyone.

"But you said you were buying a pack at Seven-Eleven," David said.

"That's where I meet the person who gets them for me. I was buying water."

David said, "Oh. Okay." Then he added, "Do I freak you out?"

It came out like he was just checking the time. "No," I said.

"It's okay if I do," David said. "I mean, it's okay if you feel like I do. Sometimes people just rub other people the wrong way. At my last job I had this supervisor, Brenda? And man, even at the interview she looked at me like I reeked or something. Everyone else was cool, and she was never an outright bitch or anything, but man, as far as I was concerned, she was not having it. Maybe it was pheromones or something. My hair was longer then, though, so maybe that was it."

"It's not you," I said.

"Okay. Just checking."

"Do I freak *you* out?"

"Oh, absolutely," he said over his shoulder.

"Splendid."

David turned to face me. "You're surprised? Everyone knows something's up. It might help if we knew what it was."

"Help *what*?"

David face tightened, and I could see him trying not to say something extraordinarily rude. "Help make shifts with you not so damn tense? I don't know."

I couldn't think of a response to that. I'd only been working here a few months, but I knew David was right. People didn't enjoy working with me.

So to escape, I said, "Is there anyone in the purple room?"

David gazed at me for a moment in silence, like he wanted to ask me something else. Then instead he just said, "No, huh-uh."

"I'm gonna mop it."

"Now?"

"Yeah."

He pressed his lips together and turned back to his tai chi book. I wanted to ask him what it was about. Instead, feeling both awful and grateful for the break, I walked to the back room where we kept the big yellow mop bucket. I wasn't really supposed to do this now. Mopping was more of an end-of-shift thing. But it was something to do. Eli wasn't the best at scheduling. We wouldn't get the next rush until about 7 p.m., right before our weekly poetry open mic. I'd be home before then. I didn't work nights.

The Hole in the Wall sits in an old residential neighborhood in downtown Phoenix, about a mile from my condo. Most of the houses around here have been torn down, but a few—like the Hole—were renovated into businesses. Eli kept many of the rooms in the little one-story building, and designed each one with its own sort of personality. One was painted purple with glow-in-the-dark stars stuck all over it. Another one, he painted red and hung old '50s monster movie posters all over. That sort of thing. Quirky indie snarky pop-culture coffee.

I'd been a little surprised Eli had hired me, since I was only sixteen, but then I found out David was seventeen, and he'd been there more than a year. A record for an indie coffee shop, as far as I knew. Eli couldn't pay a lot. It was the kind of place you worked at just to say you worked there. Quirky indie snarky street cred, I guess.

I mopped the purple room slowly, thinking about David. I did like him, actually. He was a good guy. Of all the baristas, I got along with him best. Still, he was right—I'd been pretty bitchy to him when I got here. Probably I should talk to him about that. Apologize. The other baristas wouldn't have responded quite so kindly.

By the time I was done mopping, everything inside me was back to normal, for whatever that was worth. I emptied and returned the bucket, washed my hands, and went back to the counter. Sunlight filtered through the picture window by the front door, turning the red-and-white checked curtains into fire.

"So, um . . . sorry about . . . earlier," I said as I joined him.

David's face registered interest, but he didn't look up from his book. "It's okay," he said. "Feeling better?"

"Yeah. Thanks." I paused. "You don't freak me out."

David snorted a laugh. "I'm touched. Deeply. So you want to talk about it? And if not, can you just politely say 'No, thanks, not right now' and we'll move on?"

David might've been best at putting up with me, but he wasn't a doormat. I didn't mean to be a bitch, and I didn't even think I was one most of the time. I just didn't know how to explain what went on in my head, my chest, my stomach, when I panicked. And how often and absurd it all felt.

"I get scared," I said. Just to see how it sounded. And it sounded weak. As in, pathetic. Not nearly accurate enough.

David looked up from his book. "Of what?"

"Oh, you know," I said, grabbing a rag and rinsing it out in the sink to give me something to do. "Everything."

David inhaled. About to ask more. Stupid, stupid, stupid, why did I ever open my stupid mouth?

Thankfully, I heard a car pulling into the dirt lot right then.

"You want this one?" I asked David to cut him off.

"Actually, I'm going to take my break now that you're here," David said. "You're on your own, Maverick."

I scanned what we could see of the café. The few customers

we did have were in other rooms. From here behind the counter, the café appeared empty.

"Splendid," I said.

David chuckled, like my mood amused him, then headed for the back room.

An older guy and young girl came into the shop as David disappeared. I tried to twist my face into a customer-service smile.

"Hi," I said as my cheeks cramped. "What can I get for you?"

The old man—old to me, anyway—smiled. I didn't like it. Maybe "smile" is the wrong word.

Leer. That's it. He leered at me. I think. It reminded me of the guy in the store today who'd been looking at me, glancing over and over again—

I snapped my rubber band against my wrist. I didn't need another attack while waiting on a customer. Where would I go? How could I escape? I couldn't leave the register, just bolt outside again, what if—

Snap, snap, snap. Once, twice, three. The band stung my wrist, and I winced.

"Are you all right?" the old man asked me.

The leer disappeared. I'd imagined it. He only looked concerned now. His voice was warm, his expression grandfatherly.

Pelly, I told myself, *shut up. Focus.*

"Yes," I said. "Fine. I'm sorry. You caught me napping."

I managed a weak laugh. The old man smiled and gave me an understanding nod.

"I'd like a small decaf," he said, perusing our pastry case. "And she'll have a large hot cocoa."

I studied them both as I started making the cocoa. I figured the guy to be in his fifties, maybe. Balding, starting to whistle now while jingling his keys in the pocket of his nondescript khakis. *Jang, jang, jang.* Whereas the dad carried a belly over the waist of his khakis, his daughter was one skipped meal away from being a skeleton. Her skin nearly glowed in the low light of the café. I wanted to wash her hair for her. Which I guess was ironic. It ran in long brown strings down her shoulders, with flakes of dry skin along the center part. It almost bugged me the way he ordered for his daughter, but she didn't look capable of ordering for herself.

I suppose I had no room to judge.

"Do you want any flavoring?" I asked her over the counter while I steamed the milk. Flavoring cost extra, but I wouldn't charge her for it. I just felt like doing something, anything, to brighten her day. I *felt* like she *looked*, a lot of the time. Insubstantial, skeletal, broken. It was too much like gazing into a psychic mirror. I wondered if that's how my parents or Dr. Carpenter—or David—saw me.

The girl hadn't lifted her head since she and her dad walked in. Now, when I spoke to her directly, she did. Barely. Something about the way her thin shoulders sagged and cheeks sank in made my ribs ache.

And when our eyes met, I felt all the breath in my lungs get vacuumed out like I'd been launched into outer space.

Suffocating, I choked out one word:

"*Tara?*"

The girl's dull blue eyes widened, ever so slightly, as if in shock. It couldn't have been any less shock than I was experiencing. Shock, fear, goose bumps—

I was looking at a ghost.

I hadn't seen Tara in six years.

No one had.

TWO

The girl quickly dipped her head back down, letting her greasy hair fall across her face.

"Beg pardon?" her dad said, moving to stand between the girl and the counter, blocking my view.

Except it was not her dad.

Tara's father, Michael Jacobs, looked like a movie star, tall with a prominent chin and blazing brown eyes. This guy looked more like—like Santa Claus, if anyone.

"Um . . . I'm . . . sorry," I stuttered, almost spilling the hot cocoa all over myself. "I just—she looked really familiar . . ."

"Well, her name's Leslie," the guy said, smiling. "You must've been mistaken, hmm?"

I stared at the girl again, who stood with toes pointed in, arms forming a figure 4, gripping her left elbow with her right hand, shoulders hunched. I could only see her profile.

I hurriedly poured his decaf, burning my hand with a spill. I shoved the cup across the counter toward him. My hands were starting to chill, my arms to tremble.

Here we go. Here it comes.

"That's six, um, six-forty-one," I babbled. I watched the girl as best I could, but the guy kept himself positioned between the counter and her so I couldn't see her clearly.

"You okay?" he asked me. "You look a little peaked. Should I call someone?"

"Hmm-mm," I said, shaking my head.

"You don't seem well," the man said.

"Fine," I said. "I'm fine. It's fine."

He shrugged his eyebrows and handed over a ten-dollar bill. "Keep it," he said, like the extra tip would help me regain my breath.

I couldn't take the bill. Couldn't reach toward him. Come to think of it: couldn't breathe, either. My heart screamed, *Let me out, let me OUT!*

The old man, still studying me, dropped the ten on the counter and pushed it toward me with his fingers. Then he handed the cocoa to his daughter, took her free hand, and walked to the door.

"Have a nice day," he said. "Hope you feel better."

I watched them go, not responding. Wanting to scream. *Stop, let her go, that's Tara, don't do it again—*

Tara looked back at me. Just once. Glanced sideways as the old man dragged her along behind.

Her lips moved silently, like a fish out of water. Then she was gone, out the door and into the dirt parking lot of the Hole in the Wall.

Help me?

Is that what she said? Help me . . . ?

I had to get out.

Go, get out of this space, but not outside, can't go outside, that's where *he* is, oh God, I'm trapped . . .

Tara. That was Tara. Pelly, go, do something! Don't let it happen again!

I pulled myself along the counter, dragging my cast-iron feet to the window. Literally, I could not lift my feet, only slide them along the brown concrete floor. Yanking back the curtains, I watched the guy open the passenger door of a shiny white sedan and escort the girl into the passenger seat. After shutting the door, he hitched his pants and came around the back end, went to the driver's seat, and got in.

I squinted to study the white car while my lungs shrank and my mouth dried.

Not again, not again, he's taking her again . . .

Arizona plate. Blue bumper sticker, white design—something like the Olympics logo. Four doors. Tinted windows.

The car drove out of the lot and turned onto McDowell, the major street beside the café, and headed east.

David arrived as I shoved my way back behind the counter again and wrote down all the information I'd just memorized.

"So, Pelly—" he started.

"Shh!" I hissed at him. I began with the license plate: "J, F, A . . ."

David fell silent, leaning against the counter again as I wrote. After I'd finished, I stared at the information. So paltry. Didn't even get the make or model of the car.

"So you're doing what, exactly?" David asked when I'd stopped writing. The pencil fell out of my fingers and clattered on the concrete floor.

"Not now, can't, no, just, wait," I said, picking up the café phone and dialing.

"Pelly—"

"Shh!" I said, and gripped the black phone with both hands. I felt if I let go, I'd fall to the floor.

The line picked up. "911, what is your emergency?"

"I need to, I need to report a, uh, a missing person," I stuttered. "Um, I mean, a found person. A missing . . . um, I found someone who is missing?"

"Ma'am, calm down," the operator said. "Tell me what's going on, are you in danger?"

"No! No, I—"

"Is someone there in danger?"

"No, no, it's not like that, please—"

"I'm sending a unit to you now," the operator cut in. "Tell me what is happening."

I shut my eyes and forced myself to take a breath. I wanted a smoke. Mostly I closed my eyes because I didn't want to see whatever expression David might have had. I must've sounded like a lunatic.

Which was only fair since I was crazy. We could ask my psychiatrist. Oh, wait.

I snapped my rubber band against my wrist. *Snap!* Stop intrusive thought. *Snap!* Stop intrusive thought.

"I saw my best friend Tara Jacobs," I said slowly into the phone as my tongue seemed to double in size. "She was kidnapped—I mean, she was *believed* to be kidnapped six years ago. I just saw her at my work."

It wasn't easy to ignore the look of shock on David's face when I said that. My eyes must've opened after all. Did I have any control over *anything*?

"Six years ago?" the operator said. I heard doubt in her voice.

"I know, I know how it must sound," I said, rubbing my forehead. My palm left a cold, moldy handprint. "But really, I recognized her and she said 'Help me.' She was with this old guy—"

"She asked for help?"

"Yes! Well—sort of."

"Ma'am," the operator said, sounding like an exasperated first-grade teacher, "is there an emergency at your location?"

"Well, they got into this car and drove off. I have the license plate. They can't be far away."

"You saw someone forced into a car."

This wasn't going to work.

"No," I whispered. "No one was forced into a car."

"Ma'am, when the officer gets there, you can give him a statement."

"Okay," I said as embarrassment threatened to suffocate me. Just what I needed for my next performance review with Eli: *randomly summons police to store.*

I hung up the phone and leaned against the sink, folding my arms over my belly and refusing to look at David. I didn't need to be looking at him to know he was staring at me.

"Well," David said after about a minute of silence, "that was fun."

I didn't respond. My panic started to ease, only to be replaced by helplessness. Uselessness.

"You want to tell me what's going on?" he asked.

"Not especially."

"Cops are here," David said a moment later.

Great.

THREE

"We received a call about a missing person?" the patrolman said when he got to the counter. The tag on his shirt said "Collins."

"Yes, that was me," I said while David pretended to clean the espresso machines. I hated having this conversation in front of him.

"Tell me what happened," Collins said.

I took a breath. I felt in control, but the proximity of a uniformed cop completed the cycle spinning in my head. Tara, the mall, cops, her parents . . .

"Six years ago, my best friend Tara and I were at Central Mall with her mom," I said. "We were ten. She let us go off together to Macy's, and we started chasing around, playing hide-and-seek. That kind of thing. Just being stupid. I mean,

I know you don't really play hide-and-seek when you're ten, it wasn't like that, we were just messing around—"

"Mm-hmm?"

I had told this story so many times six years ago, and I had relived it so often, it had become a soliloquy.

"So, at one point, I was hiding near these sweaters. Argyle sweaters. And then . . ."

Both Officer Collins and David stared at me, waiting for me to finish.

"Then nothing," I said. "She just never came looking for me. So I finally went looking for her mom, but she hadn't seen Tara either. We looked everywhere. Then we really got worried, and got the mall security involved, and then finally the police, but by then it had been at least an hour since anyone had seen her. People were coming and going that whole time, so there weren't really any witnesses. They checked the security tapes and found her going outside the store, waiting for a second, then jogging off into the parking lot. That's all they had. That's the last time anyone saw her."

David's eyebrows wrinkled together. That sort of felt nice. Like he cared.

"So today, this old guy showed up with this girl, and she just . . . it was her, it was Tara. I don't know who the guy was, but it wasn't her dad."

"How did you recognize her after six years?"

I licked my lips. "A mole. She had—she has a mole on her neck. It was still there. Plus she said 'Help me.' As they were leaving. He was practically pulling her out of here, and she looked back at me and said 'Help me.'"

"You're sure about that?" Collins said.

"Pretty sure, yeah. I mean, she didn't *say* it, say it. Just mouthed it. You know, so the guy wouldn't hear her."

Officer Collins didn't look impressed. And even David turned away for a second.

"I'm not lying!" I shouted. "It was Tara."

"Did they order anything?" Collins asked me.

"Yes! A decaf coffee and a hot chocolate."

"Did he use a credit card? Do you have the receipt?"

"No . . . no, he paid cash." I scanned the counter, trying to find the ten-dollar bill he'd passed to me. I didn't see it anywhere.

"He did, he paid with a ten. . . ." I started fishing through my own pockets.

That's where I found it. I must've shoved it in there when I grabbed the phone. I pulled the rumpled bill out of my hip pocket and showed it to the cop as if it were proof. As he eyeballed me, I realized what it must look like.

Like I was making up the entire thing.

"Listen," I said. "I didn't ring up the order right away, because I had to get the license plate. Look, here, see? I wrote it down. You can run the plates, can't you? I watched them get into this car. A white car, and he practically shoved her inside."

"So she was struggling?" Collins asked.

My chin tilted down. "No," I whispered, because that was

the truth. The guy had kept a hand on her the whole time, but had Tara actually struggled? Not really.

Oh God, this was not looking good.

"They can't have gotten too far," I said. "Can't you put an APB out or something?" I wasn't even sure what that meant exactly, other than "all persons bulletin" maybe, and it was something the cops always did on TV when they were looking for someone.

Collins flipped his notebook shut and tucked his pen into his breast pocket. "I'll call this in," he said. "See what the sergeant wants to do about it. It'll get sent to the detective in charge of the case."

"Larson," I said. "Detective Larson. I remember him. Phoenix Police Department."

"So it'll go to him, if he's still working here," Collins said. "And he'll probably give you a call. All right?"

"Uh-huh," I said. I sounded like a nutjob.

Collins turned to David. "Did you see anything?"

David glanced at me. I read everything he wanted to say and couldn't in that short moment: *I wish I'd been here. I wish I could say yes, I saw the whole thing.*

"No," David said. "No, I was in the back. It was all over by the time I got here."

Officer Collins nodded, then got my description of the car and the license plate, and took down all my contact information. He then walked outside talking into his radio. David slid over to me.

"So, ah . . . you going to bring me up to speed?" he asked. "What happened in here?"

"You heard me," I grouched at him. "There's nothing else to tell."

"Oh," David said. "Okay. Well, cool. I'll just tell Eli you made an emergency call and brought the police screaming down onto his business, and you can explain it all to him."

I tried to shoot David an evil glare, but evil glares weren't in my repertoire. Plus I knew David well enough to know he'd never really tell our boss.

I stared at the scrap of paper with the license plate and other info written on it. "That girl who came in," I said. "She's a friend of mine. It *has* to be her."

"She was kidnapped," David said.

"Yeah. I haven't seen her in six years."

"So . . . what happened? I mean, back then. What went on? Was there an investigation and all that?"

"Oh yeah. One minute she was there, outside the doors. Then someone must have lured her to his car, scooped her up . . . and that's it."

"Wow," David said again, searching my eyes with his. I'm not sure why.

"It took a while to figure out that she was gone," I said. "When I found her mom, she was only mad that Tara was hiding, at first. It must've been twenty or thirty minutes before we figured out something might be really wrong. So the search was just limited to the store, then the mall. I mean, by the time the cops were actually involved, it had been hours. They looked for years. The whole thing was even on one of those missing persons shows. *Abducted*. I don't think it's on anymore. . . ."

I only kept talking because I didn't like the way David's expression had shifted. Like he wasn't really listening.

"It must have really hurt you," he said.

I guess he was listening after all. Except he was hearing things I wasn't saying. I didn't like it.

"I'm over it," I said.

"*Really*," David said, but it wasn't a question.

"Really," I said, and turned back to start rewashing the sink. Just to have something to do other than look into his face.

"*So* over it that when a girl comes into the shop and reminds you of her, you write down the license plate of the car she got into and call 911?"

"It was her, goddammit, it was Tara, and I just stood here and didn't—"

I cut myself off. He wouldn't understand.

"Hey, Pelly?" David said.

"What."

"I'm sorry. Seriously."

I ground my teeth for a few seconds, then finally grunted, "Thanks."

"So what are you going to—"

"Customers," I said, pointing to the door just as a couple of business-exec types came walking in. "Slumming it," as David liked to say, for a caffeine hit.

David gave me a look like the conversation wasn't over, but I knew it was. I knew it because I decided it. I didn't want to go into it anymore. I just wanted to be better. Normal. Like it never happened.

Except it did.

And now the only places I ever went anymore were less than a mile from home. Now my only friends were psychos like me or anonymous Internet denizens. Or, sort of, David. But not really.

I snapped my rubber band against my wrist.

Stop intrusive thoughts. Stop intrusive thoughts.

FOUR

"Watch!" my little brother, Jeffrey, said as soon as I opened the front door. "Watch what I can do, Pelly!"

I had picked up the nickname Pelly from Jeffrey. When he was littler, he couldn't make all the right syllables of Penelope. Tara and I both thought it was endlessly cute.

I didn't know what I thought of it anymore.

Jeffrey sat parked in front of our TV playing some game. I didn't recognize it beyond it being on regular rotation during his school's winter break. Since Jeffrey wasn't insane, he got to go to regular school. He'd never understand how lucky he was to be able to go without a complete psychological meltdown.

I'd love to go back. I'd love to go back and complain about homework or roll my eyes at dumb teachers or have cafeteria drama. It's quite the messed-up little dynamic I've got: I don't want to be there, with all those people, all the buildings, noise . . . but I *want* to want to. It's partly the reason I stopped taking my meds and quit going to see Dr. Carpenter. Just wanted to be normal again. If I ever was.

"That's great, dude," I said, not looking at whatever it was Jeffrey was trying to get me to watch.

I walked into the hall and toward my room, catching Jeffrey frowning at me as I went. That hurt.

When I got into my room, I plugged my phone in to recharge right away. I really needed to be better about doing that. What if there was some kind of emergency, and my stupid battery wasn't charged? What if, say, someone tried to grab me?

I sat on my bed, staring cross-eyed at my peach-colored carpet. Would a cell phone have made any difference six years ago? I didn't get one until I was thirteen. That day at the mall, who would I have called, really? And if Tara had had one, whoever grabbed her would've just taken her phone, of course.

It's not "whoever," I thought. *It's that guy from the shop today. It's him.*

Tension tied my shoulders taut. It was time.

I took the white pillbox out of the coin pocket of my jeans and set it on my pillow. The light blue pillowcase needed washing. I crossed my right ankle over my left knee and rolled up my pant leg. Six-year-old posters from boy bands long since dead or turned into actors stared down and watched me. I ran a finger over the ladder of raised scars on my calf. Frets on a flesh guitar, half an inch apart. Counted them, over and over, one two three four five six seven eight, one two three four . . .

I popped open the pillbox and took out my razor. Held it up to my eye. Beyond, out of focus, my pink walls looked smudged and dingy. Thought, *Maybe I should paint them,* as I checked the blade for blood. Clean, as always. I pulled my small travel bottle of rubbing alcohol out of my backpack. Poured a capful, dipped one tip of the blade into it. Poured the capful back into the bottle. Screwed it shut. Put it away. Held my breath—

"Pelly!"

Jeffrey knocked on my door. The kid's polite, I'll give him that. Mom just barges in. When she's home.

"What," I snapped, rushing to put the blade back into my case and rolling down my pant leg. I didn't want him to know.

"Dad's on the phone," Jeffrey said through the flimsy wood. "He wants to know why you didn't call him back."

"My battery was dead," I said. "I didn't know he called. I'll call him later."

"But he's on the phone *now.*"

"Dude! Forget it, okay? I said I'll call him back."

Jeffrey made a disapproving little noise, the same kind Mom makes. That didn't help persuade me. I heard him mumbling to Dad as he went back down the hall. "Well, *I* don't know what her big *problem* is . . ."

I breathed out. That was close. I didn't want Jeffrey to see me slice. I could never explain it. It would freak him out.

What does that tell you? Dr. Carpenter's voice asked in my head.

"Shut up," I whispered. I'd already given up my meds and visits to her office. I needed my smokes and blade to get through the damn day. I'd wait until Jeffrey went to bed tonight, though. Just to be safe.

I turned my phone on while it was still charging, and found the voice mail icon shining at me. So Dad *did* call. Whatever.

My dad's an airplane pilot for a mail company. He must love his job a lot because he's always flying. Or maybe he just didn't like being home because he'd have to deal with me—

Snap! Stop intrusive thought.

My rubber band broke. Oh well. I had a drawerful. I saved every rubber band from our newspapers.

I opened my laptop and logged on to my high school site. Even taking classes all online, I was falling behind again already. I rushed through three response posts in my history class without doing the reading. Every other high school was on winter holiday break—didn't I get one too? No. I had to schedule one to have one. I hadn't done that.

My phone rang. Probably Dad. I checked the screen and saw that the number was local and that I didn't have it assigned to anyone. Who—

Then I remembered. I picked up.

"Hello?"

"Penelope Wells?"

"Yes?"

"This is Detective Larson, Phoenix Police Department."

"Yeah, hi," I said, feeling like an idiot. "Thanks for calling."

"You bet," Larson said, and I immediately remembered why I'd liked him. Or at least, not been totally afraid of him when I was ten. He had a great, deep voice that sounded like he was in control of everything around him. That had been really helpful when I was answering his questions back then.

"Why don't you run me through what happened this afternoon?" Larson went on. I imagined him flipping open a notebook.

I took a deep breath to collect my thoughts, then replayed the entire scenario for him. He said "Uh-huh" and "Okay" a lot.

"So what now?" I said when I'd finished. "Can you find the guy by his license plate or something?"

"We're taking a look," Larson said, which could have meant anything. "What I'd like to do is have you come down to my office and check out some photos, see if you can identify the guy again."

"Okay. Right now would be hard . . ."

"No, no, tomorrow is fine," Larson said. "I'll be here all day."

"Okay."

"Now, Penelope," he went on, "I'll have some other pictures for you to look at. Some people find it a little difficult."

"Pictures of what?"

"Of what Tara might look like today," he said. "Age-enhanced photos."

Something dropped from my throat into my stomach.

"Um. All right." My voice sounded weird. Quiet.

"I know it might be strange," Larson said.

"It's okay," I said. "I'm sure it'll . . . help."

"All right. We'll see you tomorrow, then."

"Um, sir? Do you believe me?"

"You mean, do I believe you saw Tara today?" Larson said. "I don't *dis*believe it. But Penelope, I have to tell you, these types of breaks are extremely rare, and even more rarely do they pan out."

"So you don't believe me. Just say that."

I said it real bitchy, even though I didn't exactly mean to. But Detective Larson didn't sound mad when he replied. I probably didn't rate high on his list of badasses.

"I *hope* you're right," he said. "I really want you to be. And I'm going to follow up on this as far as I can. If that was Tara you saw, then we'll get her back. If it wasn't . . . well, you never know."

"Okay," I said. "I'm sorry."

"No no, don't be sorry. You saw something suspicious and you called us. That's all that matters. You did the right thing."

"What about her parents? Are you telling them?"

His hesitation told me all I needed to know. But he finally said, "Maybe not just yet. We'll see where your information takes us."

"Okay," I said again. "Thanks."

"Thank you, Penelope."

Detective Larson hung up, and I turned my phone back off.

No one was going to call me, except maybe Dad again. I wasn't in the mood to talk to him, anyway.

Nor was I in the mood to deal with Mom when she came home from work. But I had to get dinner ready. It was one of my chores. Mom and Dad had agreed that since I wasn't spending time coming and going to school, then I should help out more around the house. Well, that, and that being a nutjob didn't excuse me from pitching in. I didn't mind too much. I kind of found it helpful sometimes. Distracting.

Mom came slouching into the condo like usual. She dropped her bag onto the floor with a dramatic sigh.

"How was work," she said, by rote, as she passed the kitchen.

"Awful," I called back.

I didn't hear a response, just Jeffrey shouting "hi" to her and Mom groaning "hi" back.

Swell.

Mom sells real estate, and the past year or so, she's been working a lot more. And that's my fault. When I said I *partly* went off meds and stopped seeing Dr. Carpenter because I wanted to go back to school someday . . . well, this is the other part.

Mom and Dad don't know that I heard them talking about it. About how much the sessions with Dr. Carpenter were costing. About the meds. That Dad's insurance for me had stopped. With Dad traveling so much and Mom working so much, they hadn't noticed yet that I wasn't seeing Dr. Carpenter anymore.

I'd explain it to them when they figured it out. Until then, it was my job to get better. Or if not better . . . under control. A little blood, some cigarettes, and a red-raw wrist were cheaper therapy, I figured.

I started making dinner. About the only thing I knew how to make was pasta, unless cereal counts as "cooking." I suppose there are two ingredients, so that's something.

Good thing, too, because that's what Jeffrey decided he wanted for dinner. "Frosted Flakes," he said, sliding into his chair at the table.

"Dude, you can't have Frosted Flakes for dinner," I said as I went through the work of preparing pasta sauce. This included opening the jar.

"Tough shit," Jeffrey said. "I want Frosted Flakes."

"That's a real pretty mouth you got there," I told him, and got out the cereal. He wanted sugar, let him eat sugar. I wasn't his mom.

Speaking of whom, she made her first appearance in public just as I was getting out the milk.

"You can't have cereal," she said automatically.

"See?" I said to Jeffrey.

"Why not?" he wanted to know. "There's wheat. Milk. Corn. That's *healthy*."

Mom turned to me, pleading. I stared back. "He's your kid."

"You're my kid too."

"I wasn't sure you'd noticed."

Mom grabbed the back of a kitchen chair. "Jesus God

Almighty," she said. "What crawled into your asshole today, Penelope? Today being so unique compared to other days, of course."

I looked at the floor. Want to talk about cutting? Mom's voice was sharper than my blade.

"I'm so sorry," she said, sighing. "That was rude. I've had a long day. What's the matter?"

"She's a psycho is the matter," Jeffrey muttered.

"Out," Mom said right away. "Ten minutes."

"Uhhh!" Jeffrey groaned, but carried himself into his room. It wasn't a time-out, that wouldn't work. It was just a Get Jeffrey Out of Our Hair–out. He could play games, listen to music, whatever. He just couldn't come out of his room. It was about as strict as Mom and Dad got.

"Well?" Mom asked me after Jeffrey was gone.

"So, you get to say 'asshole,' and Jeffrey can call me—"

"Yes," Mom said with a tired grin. It didn't stick. "He shouldn't call you that."

"Thanks," I said, but I'm not sure Mom heard.

"So now what's going on with you?" Mom asked.

I hadn't lifted my eyes. "I need a ride tomorrow."

"To work?" Mom asked, putting the cereal away. "What's wrong with walking?"

"Not work," I said. "I have to go to the . . . the, um . . ."

And I couldn't finish. Couldn't reopen that wound any more than it already was. No, I'd have to call out sick to the Hole, or come in late, or something. Maybe I'd agreed too quickly to go to Larson's office. The police station was nowhere near my comfort zone.

Mom kept her eyes on me. Tired, wrinkled eyes. A crease down the middle of her forehead you could stick a nickel in. I think sometimes it would've been easier on them if it'd been me instead of Tara.

"To the what?" Mom asked.

I shook my head. I'd call a cab. "Never mind. Not important."

For one second, for just one heartbeat, it looked like she was actually going to ask me again. Pursue. Inquire. *Invest.* She hadn't done that in a while, not since I got the job at the Hole. When I told her about it, Mom had been excited, believing—as I had at the time—that it was the first step toward a normal life. But four months had passed. No sign of normal on the horizon.

The moment with Mom evaporated quickly.

"I'd appreciate it if you'd finish making dinner for your brother," she said, and walked down the hall to her room.

And I'd appreciate a back rub and fresh pack of Camels, but you don't hear me complaining. I didn't say that, of course. Mom knew I smoked, but pretended not to as long as I made an effort to pretend like I didn't.

I gave my rubber band a couple of snaps before turning back to dinner. Or what passed for dinner. Frosted Flakes sounded pretty good right then.

"Pelly?" Jeffrey said from behind me.

I screwed the lid back on the pasta sauce and put it in the fridge. "What."

"Why does she talk like that?"

"Like what."

"All bitchy."

I came very close to laughing. "Because, dude. I taught her well."

"You're not bitchy."

I came very close to crying. "Thanks."

"Pelly?"

"What."

"Why do you hate me?"

The bowl slipped from my fingers and shattered on the floor. It may as well have been my spine. "What? I don't hate you."

Jeffrey shrugged. "Whatever."

"I don't," I said. "I just—"

With those two extra words, I'd said too much. I could see the question in Jeffrey's eyes. *You just what?* And I didn't have an answer. Not one I could explain to a ten-year-old.

I left the broken dish on the floor and went to my room, closing the door behind me. I heard Jeffrey getting out the broom and dustpan—to clean up *my* mess—while I turned my phone on again. No new messages.

I happened to see David's text from earlier in the day. Decided I wouldn't have to spend so much money on a cab if I was willing to deal with a little potential awkwardness, and if it wasn't bitchy of me to even ask.

So I sent a text to David. *Could you maybe give me a ride to the police station tomorrow before work? I will pay for gas.*

It took him fifteen minutes to reply. Probably he was think-ing it over as opposed to not getting the text right away. But then again, I didn't know what he did outside of work. School, I guess, but what else? And school was out for break anyway.

Maybe, he finally wrote. *What time?*

Any time that works for you, I wrote back.

Another ten minutes went by. Maybe he was talking it over with his girlfriend. If he had one. Did he?

Noon okay? he wrote at last. *Don't worry about gas.*

That's great thank you very much I appreciate it, I wrote.

I really needed to be nicer to him.

FIVE

David thought Jeffrey was hysterical. *Just what I needed.* He was even nice enough to agree to drop Jeffrey off at a friend's house, which is where Jeffrey usually spent his days during school breaks. David and Jeffrey liked the same video games, of course, and compared notes all the way to this kid Liam's house.

"Are you picking me *up*, too?" Jeffrey asked excitedly as he climbed out of David's rust-encrusted red Chevy pickup. The Chevy sounded like it had a lawn mower engine under the hood. Or maybe a Weedwacker.

David looked at me. I shrugged. "It's your car."

"Totally," David said right away. "We'll see you later this afternoon, man."

Jeffrey's face lit up with pride. No longer merely *little guy*, or *dude*, or *little bro*. He was *Man*. Like the big kids. Plus David said it with such ease and casualness, like he really was talking to one of his best friends or something.

Liam was the only ten-year-old I'd ever seen with a Mohawk. I shouted "hi" to him through the window. I owed Liam a lot. Not that he knew that. Me and Mom had brought Jeffrey to Liam's birthday party a while back, and watching all those kids . . . it made me realize it'd been six years since I'd had a real party of any kind, or even been to one. That night I started forming what would eventually become the Hole in the Wall Plan of Salvation and Normalcy.

Not the kind of thing I could or wanted to explain to a ten-year-old.

David waited until Liam opened the front door and let Jeffrey in before pulling away from the sidewalk.

"You're real lucky," I said as I watched my brother go into Liam's.

"What makes you say that? Not that I disagree."

"I don't know. Just that . . . nothing."

What I didn't say was, *You're lucky you can just be cool with my brother like that. I've never had it and never will.*

God. I was jealous of David. How did that happen?

I felt him looking at me, studying. I kept my face aimed at the window. Watching Phoenix go by. We headed toward downtown.

We both let a few minutes pass in silence before David said, "So what's going to happen today?"

"At the police station?"

"Yeah."

"I'm not sure. Looking at photos, I think. Of the guy. And age-enhanced pictures of Tara."

David must've heard something in my voice that I didn't mean to let out, because his tone dropped. "You were really good friends."

I managed a strained nod, nothing else. And snapped my rubber band.

"I hope they find her," David said a minute later.

Nod. *Snap.*

I'm not sure myself whether I meant for my silence to be a hint. David took it as one and didn't say anything else until we pulled up to the police department. Once we did, somehow the truth of how I'd been acting toward him seeped in. Guilt made my stomach burn.

"Thanks for driving me, David," I said as he pulled into a parking space.

I hated myself for the fact that he looked surprised. "It's no problem," he said. "Of course, I'll be wanting something in return."

"Um. Okay. Like what?"

"You like Will Ferrell?"

"The actor?"

"No, the dictator-of-Uganda Will Ferrell. Yes, the actor."

"Um. I guess."

"Does he make you laugh?"

"I don't know."

"Does *anything*?"

"I forget," I said. And then: laughed. Not a lot, barely a chuckle, but no mistaking it.

David actually smiled. "Okay, you realize you just laughed when you said that."

"Yeah. I'm pretty much a fruit basket."

"Fair enough," David said. "So, that's what I wanted."

My surprise laugh stopped as quickly as it had started. "I don't get it."

"Just for you to laugh, or at least relax," David said. "I mean, I'm sorry if I made you feel bad at all yesterday. I didn't know about your friend. No one does. I didn't tell anyone either, by the way . . ."

"Thank you."

"You're welcome. But I think people should know. I wish you could just take it easy, you know?"

"Yes," I said. "I do know. I'll see what I can do."

"You want me to wait out here?" David asked.

He'd do it too, I realized. He wasn't just saying it. If I wanted to go alone, he'd let me. He'd wait out here, in a cold car, until I came back. I didn't deserve that kind of sacrifice.

"Actually," I said, "I wouldn't mind a friend right now."

Something in his eyes tweaked, like he was suspicious. Then he nodded once and said, "You bet," and we got out of the car.

I hadn't wanted a friend in years. Not apart from people on message boards and whatnot. Figures the first time I actually invite someone in, so to speak, it's David Harowitz. Barista, video game geek, and chauffeur extraordinaire. Well, he looked nice today, anyway. I don't mean he was dressed up, because he wasn't. But the right T-shirt makes all the difference, you know? Maybe he had plans later.

Snap.

Get in the game, Pelly, I thought. *Focus. Get Tara back so that you can . . .*

"I've been meaning to ask you, what's up with the rubber band?" David asked as we neared the imposing glass doors of the police department.

"Oh, it's a reminder thing," I said. David opened the door for me. "Thanks. It's supposed to remind me to change my thought pattern."

"From what to what?"

A blast of warm air smelling mostly like Clorox but a little like pee rushed out to meet us. Like a kindergarten classroom without the comforting scents of Crayolas and paste. I flinched. It was the exact same smell as six years ago.

"Anything to anything else," I said, dodging the question. Maybe I could count on David to drive me all over town or come into a police department with me. That didn't mean I was going to drag him into my emotional toilet.

We checked in at the front desk and got directions to Detective Larson's desk. It hadn't moved. I wasn't sure whether it was a good or bad thing that everything was the same as the last time I came here.

Larson met us at the entrance to the big room full of cubicle desks where other detectives were on phones, talking to people or each other, or, in one case, sleeping.

"Thanks for coming by," Larson said after I introduced David. "Come on in here."

He led us into a small conference room with a folding table and a few folding chairs. We sat opposite him. Larson got right to work, handing me a sheet of color headshots. They all looked like driver license photos.

"Can you pick out the man you saw yesterday?"

I appreciated that he didn't phrase it like "the man you *think* you saw." That might've broken me in half. I studied the six photos. Two of them looked like the guy I'd seen. I wasn't about to tell Larson more than one looked like him.

Larson chitchatted with David while I studied the photos. Had David seen anything; no sir, but I was working that day; did you see anything suspicious at all; no, not really, sir . . .

"This one," I said, pointing.

Larson took the paper back. "Number three?"

"Yes," I said. "That's him."

But what if I was wrong? Eli kept the Hole in the Wall pretty dark, as part of its moody, quirky indie snarky ambience.

Larson made a note. "Okay," he said. "Now, I'm going to show you—"

"Was that him?" I asked, and immediately thought, *That sounds terrible and uncertain.* "I mean, I got it right, didn't I?"

Larson waved me off. "Don't worry about that," he said.

"Even if you didn't identify the owner of the car, we're still looking into this."

"But *did* I?"

The detective's face hardened just a fraction. "Don't worry about it, Penelope," he said. He handed me several papers. "Here's some age enhancements we have of Tara. Do any of them look familiar?"

My hand shook as I took the papers from him. I saw David frowning a little as he watched me. But he was looking at my face, not my hand.

The printouts of the age enhancements were spooky. It was Tara, for sure, but—not. They seemed like high-tech caricatures; the features were right but exaggerated just a little. I went slowly through the stack, trying to merge the images with the girl I'd seen yesterday.

Merge them with *Tara*, I mean.

I'm not sure how long I'd been staring at them when Larson said softly, "What do you think?"

"I don't know," I whispered. No point in lying. "This is her. And so is the girl I saw at the coffee shop. But they're not the same."

"Not the same by a pretty wide margin, or not exactly identical?" Larson asked. "Because age enhancement is never exact. It's just an approximation."

I shook my head and gave him back the pictures. "I don't know," I said again. "But I know that girl was Tara."

Larson took the pictures and slid them into a file. "Well,

like I said, we are looking into it. We know where the car owner lives, and we're working with other agencies to see what we can find out."

"Agencies?" David said, and I immediately wished he'd shut up. "Like, the CIA?"

Larson smiled toothlessly. "No no, nothing like that. Just other law enforcement agencies."

"Are you telling her parents?" I said. "Maybe they know something, maybe they know the guy?"

"We'll bring them in when the time comes," Larson said, which was about as nice a brush-off as I'd ever heard.

"Okay," I said, defeated. My head hurt.

Larson stood up, so David and I did too. "I'll keep in touch," Larson said. "And if you think of anything else, don't hesitate to call me."

"Thanks," I said.

David and Larson traded nods, and we made our way back out the way we'd come. Once we were outside, David said, "How did that go, do you think? I couldn't tell."

"Dunno," I grumbled.

"That good, huh?"

"Whatever."

I felt him wanting to ask more, but he didn't. We walked back to the car and climbed in. It took a massive force of will for me not to slam the door. No reason to take out my frustration on his truck.

"We've got some time before work," David said hesitantly

as he pulled into traffic. "Where should we—I mean, where do you want to go?"

"Doesn't matter," I whispered.

"Pelly? Are you okay?"

"No, I'm not okay," I said. "My best friend got kidnapped and I didn't do anything about it and now she's out there somewhere and *no one*'s doing anything about it, including me, and if I could just find her and get her back then I could—"

Stop. Shut up.

I crammed my hand against my mouth to stanch the flow of words bleeding from me. I wanted to roll up my jeans right then and there. Bleed for real, bleed the hate. I'd just said more to David Harowitz about Tara than I'd told anybody since my therapist.

That shows how much I enjoyed sharing. David, however, didn't seem put off at all.

"You could what?" he asked.

"I don't know," I said. Which was a lie.

David gave me a little snort. "In other words, 'Shut up and stop bothering me, David.'"

"That's not what I meant," I said. "I just . . ."

We were at a stoplight. David took his eyes off the road and turned to me. His hazel eyes, dotted with kelly green, were so sincere I felt my resolve slipping.

I couldn't stomach looking at him. Stared out my window again instead.

"That's when it all started," I said quietly, hoping maybe he couldn't hear me and would give up listening. "When Tara got taken, everything went to hell. I got scared. Thought someone would take me, too. Or Jeffrey. I couldn't even look at him anymore. I just stayed inside. I couldn't go to school. I faked sick so much my mom thought I really had something bad, like cancer or something. And Mom and Dad didn't understand at all, I mean, they tried to, but I couldn't make them see . . ."

I stopped. The car behind us honked, and David hit the gas to carry us through the green light. He didn't say anything. Neither did I. I'd already puked out more secrets than I ever wanted to, anyway.

I zoned out, not paying attention to where we were going. When we stopped, I lifted my head and glanced around.

"Is this cool?" David asked. He'd stopped the truck, but hadn't shut off the engine yet.

We'd ended up at this little park called Arcadia. A couple of fields and a decent-size playground, plus lots of concrete picnic tables and grills.

"Um . . . sure," I said. I had no idea what we were doing here.

David shut off the engine and climbed out, and I followed. Without a word, he led us toward the empty playground. I would've thought it would be crowded since the schools were closed.

"You're on break from school, right?" I asked.

"Yeah," David said. "But I've only got about half a schedule next semester, and a terminal case of senioritis."

"So, what, you ditch a lot?"

"Actually, no, not excessively. I'm kind of a goody-goody. You?"

Oops. Hadn't meant to go quite that far. "I'm taking classes online. Ditching doesn't have quite the allure."

David looked like he wanted to ask more, but he didn't say anything else about it.

Instead he marched onto the sand and said, "Swings?"

I stayed on the sidewalk. "I don't think so."

"Whatever," he said. "You're missing out."

David slipped himself into one of the rubber seats and launched backward with both feet. In just a moment he was arcing high into the air, back and forth.

He looked ridiculous. I wanted to tell him so. Except then when I did, I also laughed. I hardly recognized the sound.

"Yes, I do look ridiculous," David said. "But at least I'm having fun. Lookit, there's five more here. You wouldn't even have to sit next to me or anything."

He didn't say it bitterly. In fact, I couldn't quite figure out how he meant it. Sarcastic? Flirty? Just a statement of fact?

So just to show him I couldn't be manipulated, I climbed into the swing beside his and pushed off. Pretty soon we were in sync, up and down, back and forth, not speaking. For no good reason I remembered suddenly in grade school, when Tara and I got into sync like this, we shouted, "You're in my bathtub!" I don't know why. It was just one of those things kids said, I guess. We'd heard other kids say it before. It always cracked us up.

Maybe because of the way my stomach kept squishing up into my ribs, then down past my belly button, I didn't feel quite as hopeless as I had at the police station. Maybe the g-forces were relaxing my guts or something.

"I'm gonna jump," David announced.

"Don't!" I said.

"Why?"

"You'll crack your skull open and your brains will fall out and I am not cleaning it up." This was a phrase my mom always used to say to me and Jeffrey. For pretty much any occasion. Jumping on the couch, climbing ladders, whatever.

"Nah. I'm gonna do it."

"David—"

And then he was airborne. A wild splay of arms and legs that I thought for sure would result in multiple compound fractures. But David landed expertly on his feet like a gymnast, and threw his fists up over his head as if to complete the image.

"Stuck the landing!" he announced.

I wanted to jump too. Instead I dragged my feet in the sand until I could hop off. "You could've been killed," I said.

"I doubt it."

"Whatever, it's your ass on the line."

David grinned. "Hey, come here," he said, and took off through the sand again.

What was I supposed to do? I followed after him, grumbling because of all the sand slipping into my sneakers.

David jumped onto a wooden deck plugged into the ground

by a giant spring. He spread his feet and bounced back and forth on the platform, making it rock.

"Awesome!" he said. He stopped bouncing and held out a hand. "Come on up."

"No," I said, taking a step back.

"Come on," David said. "I'm going to show you something."

I made a face to let him know I was suspicious, to say the least. Since I had to kill time before work anyway, I went ahead and climbed aboard.

I didn't take his hand, though. He didn't seem to notice.

"Hands up," David said, raising his own in a limp sort of way. It reminded me of a dog sitting back and begging, the way his hands curved at the wrist.

I raised my arms like a zombie.

"Geez, no, loosen up," David said. "Relax your shoulders. Bend your elbows. Let your hands float a little. See?"

"Okay . . ."

"Now just follow me," David said. He put his wrists against mine, and began moving his hands in slow circles. I was reminded of *The Karate Kid* and wax on, wax off.

"Is this some kind of dance?"

"Nope. Martial arts."

"What? Come on." Secretly I was pleased I'd sort of guessed right in my head.

"It is," David insisted. "It's wing chun. Or you can call it sticky hands. It's what Bruce Lee practiced before he created Jeet Kune Do."

"Can you say that again in American?"

"Nope," David said. "Now I'm going to move a hand toward you. You just stay attached to my wrist, okay? Go with it, but don't let me in."

"Uh . . . okay . . ."

He gently eased his right hand toward my shoulder. I resisted.

"No, relax," David said. "Blend. Blend."

"Like a milkshake?"

"Like a tree. Bend with the wind instead of trying to stand against it."

"You are making no sense."

"I know," David said. "It's a gift."

"Are you going to make me wax your car, paint your house, paint your fence?"

"I'm not that inscrutable," he said with a smile. "But I am working on it. Cultivating that whole mysterious inner peace and calm thing, yet maintaining the ability to whoop on a bunch of kids in skeleton tights . . ."

We hadn't detached our wrists through the entire conversation. He kept moving his hands, his wrists lightly touching my own. Suddenly—though not in a surprising way—he moved his right hand toward my shoulder again. I let him get close, but shifted my shoulder away and let my hand drop, taking his with it.

"Yeah," David said. "There, you got it. Nice."

I got a weird cramp in my face, and after a second I realized

I was smiling. And that I didn't want a cigarette. And that my heart was slower than it had been in the past six years without major pharmaceuticals. . . .

I stopped moving. Dropped my hands. David dropped his too.

"That was awesome," he said.

My heart sped up. I wanted a smoke.

I hopped off the platform and started heading for the car. Sand sucked at my feet, making it feel like I was walking through a swimming pool. The same sensation as I'd had yesterday at the Hole in the Wall.

"Pelly?" David called. In a moment he had fallen into step with me. "What's up?"

"What're you doing?" I said, my voice low and tight.

"Um . . . hanging out at the park?"

"Stop it." I paused and looked up at him. "What are you *really* doing?"

David's body sagged. He sort of snorted. "Trying to cheer you up, actually."

"By teaching me karate?"

"Wing chun."

"Whatever. I don't want to be *cheered up*, all right? Life sucks, and that's it. All the swinging in the world won't change that."

"Or bring her back," David said.

"*Or* bring her back, that's right!" I said. Then I blinked. "Wait, what's that supposed to mean? What are you saying?"

"Nothing," David said. He shook his head, eyes averted. Then he glared at me. "I just thought it had been a bad couple days for you, is all. And maybe you'd want to get out of your head for a while."

"There's no getting out of my head," I said, crossing my arms and staring down at the concrete.

"*Clearly*," David said, and the sharpness in his voice startled me. "Jesus, Pelly. You know, I don't even know why I bothered. You ask me for help, which I then give you, and then—and then this. This is what I get."

"I'll give you gas money—"

"What the hell, are you kidding me?" David's eyes bugged out, and he took several paces away from me as if he needed the room to use his long arms to gesture more effectively. "*Gas* money? How about just taking it easy for a minute? How about, I don't know, *smiling*?"

"I don't see anything funny here," I said.

"Well that sure makes two of us." David turned and looked out at the playground for a minute, then began walking toward the truck without waiting for me. "Let's just go."

I followed David, thinking, *Good work, Pelly. If "bitch" was an Olympic event, you'd be a medalist.* I snapped my rubber band till my wrist was red. My calves tingled in anticipation of being bled, of releasing the tension and switching my brain off.

Neither of us said anything as David drove us to the Hole in the Wall. He turned the radio on, a little loud, something playing Top 40. Then when we pulled into the dirt parking lot, my body stiffened in the seat and I sucked in a breath.

"What now?" David said.

I shook my head. Stared at the entrance. Even in broad daylight the building I'd come to appreciate as a home away from home looked like an ancient dungeon, waiting to consume me.

"I don't know if I can go back in there," I said. My stomach felt the same way it did a few years back when I started ditching school. Cramped and fluid. My chest constricted, my breath quick and tight. I swallowed and shivered, hearing the creep's keys jingling in my head.

David didn't say anything for a minute. I saw him shaking his head a little. Then he said, "Guess you better call out sick, then."

With that, he got out of his truck and shut the door, heading into the Hole. I watched him go, feeling absolutely useless and stupid and petrified. I couldn't move. Couldn't dig out my phone, or get out of the car and walk home, and I sure couldn't go to work.

So when David reappeared from the Hole a few minutes later and walked back to the truck, I assumed it was to tell me to get the hell out of it. Go walk home, or come in and go to work, but definitely and certainly get out of his truck.

He climbed in, his mouth drawn tight. "Home?" he asked.

"What are you . . . what did—"

"Told Eli you were sick and I'd take you home. But I don't

care if you actually go home or not, I'll drop you off wherever you want, I do not care."

I was not attracted to David Harowitz. But right then I came perilously close to kissing him. No one had done anything like that for me before. He was pissed, yes. And I didn't blame him. I had that effect on people. But still. He'd gone to the trouble.

"Um, sure," I said.

"Sure, what."

"I mean home, sure."

David pulled out of the parking lot without another word.

I said, "Aren't you going to get in trouble with Eli?"

"Who knows, who cares," David said. "I just like to live dangerously. I'm a real adrenaline junkie."

Clearly he was joking, but he didn't smile.

I decided silence was my best option. I watched the city go by, grateful I wasn't out in it. I wondered what Tara was doing, where she was. Truthfully, I'd hoped for more from Detective Larson. There had to be some way to make him understand I wasn't out of my mind. Or no more so than usual, anyway.

And I knew what I had to do.

"Um, David?"

"What."

"Can I ask you for another favor? And you can say no."

David barked a mirthless laugh. "Oh, *may* I?" he said. "Trust me, I know I can say no."

He ground his teeth for a couple seconds, then said, "What is it."

"Could you maybe take me up to Paradise Valley? I need to talk to someone."

"Wow," David said. "You must think I am the world's biggest pushover weenie doormat."

"No. No, it's not that."

"Well, I think I am." He switched lanes. Signaled and everything. He was a really careful driver. "I don't know why I'm doing this. Where are we going?"

I wiped my hands on my jeans. "To see Tara's parents."

SIX

Tara lived—I mean, her family lived—in a newer development where the houses looked like they'd been manufactured at some mansion factory and shipped here. You could practically walk from red-tile rooftop to rooftop. The Homeowners Association ensured every lawn was green and fresh. Every street clean and smooth. Every flower expertly clipped. A pretty place to live, I guess. But also kind of sterile.

"Nice neighborhood," David muttered.

"Yeah."

"What do her parents do?" David asked after I pointed to the next turn we needed to make.

"Her dad's an architect. Her mom teaches college classes from home. Like, online. History. That's what they did when we lost Tara, anyway. I haven't talked to them since Tara's older sister, Carla, went out of state to college. That was a few years ago now."

"Well, at least we've gotten everyone's attention," David said, kind of low, like the neighbors could hear.

I saw what he meant. David's rusty red pickup stuck out, as my mom once said about an old dress, "like a turd in the caviar." Any car older than three years in this area was cause for alarm.

"Where do you live?" I asked. For some reason I felt like I needed to know.

David shook his head quickly. "Not like this," he said, his eyes darting around at the large houses. "Not here. Not in a place like this, I mean."

He blew out a breath. I'd never seen him nervous like that before. Funny that it would take a sort of rich part of town to make him respond like that.

I had David park on the street in front of the Jacobses' house. Or what I hoped was still their house.

"What're we doing here again?" David asked as he kept glancing around the neighborhood. "I mean, what exactly is your big plan? You sure you want to open this up with them?"

"No, I'm not entirely sure," I said through closed teeth. "It's just that maybe something will trigger a memory for them, like maybe that guy used to work for her dad, or coached soccer when Tara used to play. Something. I don't know. I just know that I can't sit around waiting."

"You don't have to do it," David said. "I mean, it was spur of the moment."

"I *know*," I said, turning to stare at the house. Just seeing it again was making me chilly beneath my skin. For a moment I imagined Tara coming bounding out the front door, summer-tan and sixteen, ready to jump into a Jeep and conquer the world. I ran with her, smiling, squinting at the sun, thinking, *You can't stop me, you can't stop me.*

I sucked in a breath. I'd never been that girl. I could never *be* that girl. Not unless I got Tara back.

I sat motionless as David drew in a long breath through his nose. He still didn't look comfortable being here. But then to my surprise, he said, "So you want me to come with?"

"No," I said. "It's probably better if you wait. Do you mind?"

David shut off the engine and said, "Nope." He leaned across me and opened the glove box. He took out a book and sat back in his seat. I grabbed it away from him and looked at the title.

"*Tai Chi Classics*?" I said, recognizing it from the café. "You really are into this whole cage-fighting thing?"

"Hardly," David said. "Wing chun and tai chi don't have much to do with MMA."

"But you really do study it?"

"Sure. Since I was little. Seven or eight."

"Are you, like, a black belt or something?"

"Not exactly."

"That's cool."

"Thanks," David said. "Are you stalling?"

"Kind of."

"You okay?"

He'd been asking that a lot lately. I nodded. Let the breath out. "If it was your kid, you'd want any information that was out there, wouldn't you?"

"Probably."

"And if I tell them what's happening, they might be able to make the cops do more. Right?"

"What is it that you think the cops are *not* doing?"

"I don't know, but . . . well, you saw Detective Larson this morning. He doesn't believe me."

"That's not what I saw, Pelly."

"I mean he doesn't think anything will really come out of it, that's all," I said, squeezing my hands into impotent fists. "Not that I was, like, lying or anything. God."

"No, I—sorry," David said. He shifted around in his seat. "Well, if you're gonna go, go."

"Okay," I said. "Okay. David?"

"What."

"Thanks."

I climbed out before I could see or hear a response. I was afraid I wouldn't have liked it.

A pale brown stone path curved to the front door. I followed it, wondering if an alarm would sound if I stepped onto the grass. I rang the doorbell and waited.

Mrs. Jacobs opened the door and gazed down at me.

"Yes?"

It felt like someone had jabbed a needle into my heart. She didn't even recognize me.

"Mrs. Jacobs? It's me. Penelope Wells? Pelly?"

Her frown stayed in place for another long moment, lips drawn down, eyes tired. Finally she straightened up a bit and almost smiled.

"Pelly," she said. "My God. How are you? Come in."

Relieved, I walked into the house and Mrs. Jacobs shut the door behind me. She walked—or shuffled, really—to the kitchen. A coffee scent not as good as our Hole in the Wall blend filled the room. It smelled burnt.

"Please, sit," Mrs. Jacobs said, gesturing weakly to a kitchen chair.

I sat down and folded my hands tightly in my lap. Now that I was here, I didn't know how to tell her what I'd seen. I should have given myself time to rehearse.

"How have you been?" Mrs. Jacobs asked, sitting across from me. A laptop sat open on the table in front of her. "It's been so long."

Her forehead wrinkled when she said it, like there was more than one meaning to her words. I suppose there was. Wondered suddenly if my being there hurt her. If I reminded her too much of Tara.

Everything on the planet probably reminds her of Tara, just like everything reminds you of how things used to be and how you can't drive past that mall without looking for Tara like she'd still be—

Snap. I used my rubber band, keeping my hands under the table. Focus, Pelly. Focus.

"I need to tell you something important," I said carefully, staring at the tabletop. It was the same table as when I'd been here last. I recognized a knot and crack in the wood that reminded me of an old oak lollipop.

"And I don't know how you're going to take it," I went on. "I tried talking to the police this morning, but . . ."

Her forehead wrinkled again. I'd always thought Mrs. Jacobs was a pretty woman. Elegant and put-together. After Tara disappeared, though, day by day her appearance had deteriorated. Either her hair had turned gray or she stopped trying to cover it up, I don't know which. Fine wrinkles that had made her distinguished six years ago had grown into deep creases that didn't flatter her skin. Even her beautiful brown eyes seemed to have a film over them.

"All right," she said. "What is it? Are you in trouble?"

"Oh, no, I'm fine," I said. "It's just that . . . I got this job at a coffee shop in downtown Phoenix a few months ago, and yesterday I saw . . . Mrs. Jacobs, I saw Tara."

Her jaw went rigid, eyes unblinking.

"I know how that must sound," I added quickly. "I didn't believe it myself at first, but it was her. She had that mole on her neck and everything. She was with this old guy, this creepy older guy, and she was so pale and skinny . . ."

I babbled on and on while Mrs. Jacobs sat rock-still in her chair, staring at me.

"So I called the police, and this morning I went to the station and talked to Detective Larson, you remember him? And I ID'd the guy I saw, at least I think I did, but . . ."

I trailed off as I looked into Mrs. Jacobs's eyes.

This was a bad idea, my coming here. A terrible, horrible, no-good, very bad idea.

Mrs. Jacobs rose from her chair and walked stiffly to a cabinet near the fridge. She took out a prescription bottle, and I couldn't help but notice several others on the bottom shelf. She shook out two small pills and placed them on her tongue, then splashed them down with a half-empty glass of water nearby.

Her hands shook the entire time.

"So, yeah. That's it, that's everything," I said. I had to fill the silence. It was giving me goose bumps.

She hadn't moved since taking the pills. Just stood by the counter, gripping its edge.

"Mrs. Jacobs? Are you all right?"

"No," she growled. "I am rather *far* from all right."

I sucked in a breath and bit down on my lower lip.

Mrs. Jacobs whirled on me but kept a hand on the counter as if to steady herself.

"Six years," she said. "Six years I've waited and prayed for my little girl to come home and she hasn't. How dare you come in here saying this kind of nonsense? Penelope, how could you?"

"I'm sorry," I whispered.

"I never blamed you, I always blamed myself," Mrs. Jacobs went on as if she hadn't heard me. And it kind of looked like she hadn't. "I thought that was clear, I thought you understood that . . ."

"I did," I said, and immediately it sounded wrong. Like I was saying it *was* her fault.

"*Get out,*" Mrs. Jacobs barked, pointing a sharp finger toward the front hallway.

I dropped my head and raced out of the kitchen, out of the foyer, and out the front door, not stopping to bother closing it behind me, all but running down the stone path to David's car, climbing in, and slamming the door shut. My eyes had irised halfway shut, like tunnel vision.

"Go," I said.

David set his book aside. "How'd it—"

"Stupid," I said out loud. I was saying it only to myself.

Winter sunlight warmed the interior of the car. I gazed slowly around at the neighborhood; at the various shades of tan paint coating all the look-alike houses, the cloudless sky overhead, the shiny cars parked on pristine white carports. The Jacobs home sat in a cul-de-sac.

A dead end.

This neighborhood, the Jacobses' house, the calls to the cops. All of it.

"So stupid," I whispered.

I could feel David wanting to ask, wanting to know, wanting

to do something. Finally, he did the absolute right thing: he tossed his book under his seat, started the car, and took me home.

I didn't say thank you. But I did try.

SEVEN

I had David drop me off at home. We shared mumbled good-byes, and that was it.

I scurried into the house alone. Closed and locked the door. Rushed to my room. Sat on my bed, got my gear, bared my leg. Drew the razor north to south down my calf, close to my knee pit.

Burn, burn, burn.

My heart stopped. Considered. Started up again, slower. Slower. Slowing . . .

Better.

I cleaned the blade and put it back into its case, which went back into my pocket. I dabbed the slice with tissue from the travel-size pack I kept in my bag. Never toilet paper, never a napkin. It's got to be my own personal stash. Couldn't say why. Maybe I was afraid of germs.

Once the blood stopped draining, I plastered it with a bandage three fingers wide, rolled my pant leg back down, checked myself in the bathroom mirror, and, finally, tried to do math problems until Mom and Jeffrey would be home.

It's a lot of work being me anymore.

A few hours later, as I was trying to get something ready for dinner, Mom arrived home with Jeffrey in tow, muttering about having to leave work early to go pick him up, and why couldn't I just get my driver's license like a sensible teenager so she wouldn't have to drag not one but two of us around all the time. . . .

So instantly my mood perked up.

Just kidding.

"Why didn't that guy David come get me?" Jeffrey wanted to know as soon as he walked in the door behind Mom.

"Because he had things to do," I said, trying unsuccessfully to boil pasta for dinner.

"What kinds of things?" Jeffrey wanted to know.

"The world doesn't revolve around you!" I shouted.

Jeffrey blinked up at me, wounded. He set his jaw and said, "You suck."

He marched out of the kitchen just as Mom marched back in from dumping her bag in her bedroom.

"What on earth?" she said.

"Nothing," I said, dumping mashed pasta down the disposal. It's a mystery to me how I could fail to boil pasta correctly. I slammed the colander into the sink. "You'll have to order in."

"What is the matter with you?" Mom asked.

"What *isn't*?" I said back. "I just want to feel *better*, you know, just go back to how everything used to be, but no one will *let* me, and I miss . . . I just miss . . ."

I suppose the most logical way to finish that sentence was with the name "Tara." Only that wasn't the first thing that came to mind. The first thing that came to mind was "me."

Mom listened to all this with her eyebrows raised.

"Have you been taking your meds?" she asked. Just a polite inquiry. Just *wondering*, you know, just *curious*, no biggie either way.

"No," I said as defeat dragged my shoulders down. "No, Mom. I haven't. I got tired of being tired. I got tired of not being able to think at all."

That was no lie. Then again, thinking hadn't gotten me very far lately.

"Well, maybe they need to change them up," Mom said. "It's not an exact science, you know. Maybe you need a new dosage, or a new kind . . ."

I stared at her, long enough and in a silence so cold she couldn't miss it.

"What?" she said.

"Change the dosage," I said slowly. "Okay."

I walked out of the kitchen and into my room, ignoring Jeffrey and his video game in the living room. I closed my door, squatted on the floor, and screamed into my elbow.

After screaming for about three or four years straight, my

vocal cords as raw as rancid hamburger, I stayed hunkered on the floor, wishing for the little yellow pills my doctor had prescribed after Tara was taken. They'd usually knock me out cold, and if they didn't, I could at least spend the next six to eight hours comfortably numb to the world. That's what I wanted more than anything right then.

By the time I stood up, my knees practically creaked. I must've been down there for a while. I lost track of time on occasion. I turned on my laptop and clicked a link in my favorites folder: missingkids.com.

Ten Tips for a Safe Holiday Season

NCMEC Announces New Training

Have You Seen These Children?

Like I did every day, then every week, and eventually every month, I entered Tara's information in the search box and clicked it. Her poster gazed back at me, the school photo from fourth grade centered on the page beside one of the age-enhanced ones Larson had shown me. I'd never seen that image on this site before. Had it been that long since I had checked out her page? How long had they had an age-enhanced photo posted?

Like I said, I tended to lose track of time.

Guilt filled me up like it came from a hose jammed into my mouth. A full-pressure blast punching holes in all my digestive organs. Some friend I was.

I squinted at the photo, letting my eyes tennis-match between the fourth-grade photo and the new one. I didn't see anything new or different. Both photos were Tara, pretty much. I wished I could go back to yesterday and get one more good look at her.

I clicked the page closed and checked my phone. The low-battery indicator was already on. That reminded me of David texting me yesterday to let me know I was running late. He didn't have to do that. Eli kept a master list of everyone's cell, but we rarely used it. And David sure as hell didn't have to drive me all over town.

Except on occasion for work, I'd never texted David before. But then after yesterday at the Hole in the Wall, and today, him seeing me in all my panicky glory, it occurred to me that I didn't really have anything to hide from him.

And I didn't have to act like I did toward him at the park. That's what we used to pay Dr. Carpenter for. Ha-ha.

Dr. Carpenter had been a nice-enough woman, and I really had gotten better while I saw her. I mean, I could leave the house now, and even hold down a job, clearly. Before that I'd just stayed indoors and faked my way through my online classes, read books, watched movies, and perfected my slicing. If I hadn't seen Tara at the shop, maybe I would've made the transition from basket case to functional human being. Like I'd planned. Maybe that wasn't to be.

Dr. Carpenter couldn't bring Tara back, or change my Dad's schedule, or make my mom stop worrying about money and work all the time.

But . . .

Now, here was a new idea.

Maybe *I* could.

I reopened my browser and searched for *find license plate owner*. I brought up a whole list of sites that claimed I could look up anyone by their plate number. Most of them, no doubt, were totally bogus. I started clicking around, looking for signs of legitimacy.

I settled on a site that looked legit, and entered the info I'd kept from yesterday. I chewed my lip, waiting for the results to pop up. What I got instead was a request for fifteen bucks.

"Son of a bitch," I said.

The site glared at me from my laptop screen, wanting to know if I wished to proceed. I didn't have a credit card. I'd never really needed it. Mom or Dad made my deposits, and brought back cash for whatever. It's not like I was out partying every night.

Just a few clicks and keystrokes, and I could have the name of the man who took Tara. Information the police surely already had but would never share with me.

What harm could it do? Just to *see*. Maybe there would be something that would catch in my mental filter that the cops couldn't possibly know. Some clue, some hint. Something from that awful goddamn day at the mall that I'd forgotten about.

The scent of pizza wafted in from the kitchen. I guess I couldn't blame Mom for ordering since I'd abandoned the pasta. I wasn't hungry anyway. I debated trying to ask for, then to steal, one of her cards, but knew I'd never get her to agree and that I didn't have the guts to just take one and use it.

I saved the license plate lookup site to my favorites and shut down my laptop. I didn't remember anything else until I woke up the next morning on top of my bedspread and still in yesterday's clothes. I don't know if I had any dreams, but I knew when I woke up, staring at my ceiling, that I really needed to fix things with David.

He was the only person I could come close to calling a friend. That might be the best I could ever do if things didn't change.

EIGHT

By the time I'd showered and gotten ready for work that morning, the whole idea of trying to find Tara through a stupid license plate website seemed absurd. What on earth could I possibly do that the cops couldn't? So I'd decided to try to forget about it. *Stop intrusive thoughts* and all that. It just made me more miserable.

Plus . . .

I mean, what were the chances, *really*? Of all the quirky snarky indie coffee shops in town—in the state, in the nation—Tara and her kidnapper came to mine?

Suffice it to say, it was my worst day at the Hole, except for Wednesday. I kept waiting for Tara and that old man to come back in. So I could prove it was them. Then I waited for the old man to arrive alone, but with a gun, mowing us all down because I'd figured him out. Then I waited for Dr. Carpenter to show up with a squad of mental health goons to wrap me up and ship me back to my hospital for ever thinking I'd seen Tara at all.

I spent five hours at work with my heart pounding its fists inside me, making my sternum quake with each beat. I couldn't catch my breath. Kept dropping things. I jerked every time the door opened.

I knew that was dumb. Tara and that creepy old man weren't coming back here, because it wasn't them.

David clocked in an hour before I was scheduled to clock out. We made eye contact as he came around the counter to grab his apron.

"Hey," I said.

"Hey," he said back.

Okay, well, that was a decent start.

"I'm sorry about yesterday," I said.

"Okay." David tied on his apron, looking bored. It seemed forced, though. Like he wanted me to know how unimpressed he was so far.

"Can I—I mean, I want to make it up to you somehow if I can," I said.

"Oh yeah? Like how."

"I don't know . . . I could take a couple of your shifts or something."

"I need the money."

"Well, okay, then . . . I don't know, I'll, I'll buy you lunch or something."

He practically choked. "You're asking me out?"

"No, I'm not asking you out! I'm saying that I want to do something, you know, like dinner. Or whatever. Out to *eat*."

I snapped my rubber band, and David watched me do it.

"So I give you a hand," he said with faux thoughtfulness, "*twice*, in fact . . . you flip out on me, and then you ask me out."

"I'm not asking you out."

"Then what are you doing?"

"I'm apologizing! I want to make it up to you."

"So the apology itself isn't good enough?"

"If you say it is . . . I don't know! God! I just want to do the right thing, okay? I'm sorry!"

David didn't say anything for a minute. I moved to the sink and began washing it furiously. Stupid. It was a stupid idea. Make friends with David Harowitz, yeah, great.

"You ever hear of a place called Orange Table?"

I paused, and threw the rag aside. "No."

"It's at the Civic Center, you know where that is? By the library?"

"Okay, yeah . . ."

"They make this burger called the Arrogant Bastard," David said. "It's, like, eleven bucks. It's my favorite burger in the entire galaxy. Hook me up with one of those, and we'll call it even."

I kicked at the splash mat with one toe. "Really?"

"Really and truly."

"Okay," I said. "When's good for you?"

"How about tonight?"

"No, no, no," I said. "No. Sorry. Not at night."

"You got a date or something?" David said.

I didn't answer. He hadn't heard me correctly. Now what?

David waited for me. I couldn't read his expression.

Tonight, I thought. At night. Go out at night. I hadn't done that in years. Maybe once or twice, here and there with Mom or Dad, but it never went well. Once the sun set, my pulse doubled if I walked as far as our driveway. Someone could drive by, grab me . . .

"Tonight?" I said, but it was only a squeak. I cleared my throat. "Tonight," I said again. "Um. Sure. Okay."

I had to do it sometime. I had this job; I'd ditched my meds; maybe one night out would bring me one step closer to being able to get back to school. And that would make me normal.

"I suppose the irony here is that you'll need a ride," David said.

Shit, I thought.

"Well . . . kinda."

He sort of laughed through his nose. "So be it," he said. "I'll pick you up at seven."

"Okay," I said. I felt like saying thank you but didn't. I wasn't sure what I'd mean if I did.

It wasn't until later that I realized that everything I'd said could possibly be construed as a date, despite emphasizing that I was not asking him out.

That made for an interesting afternoon of work. But at least it kept me from thinking about the darkness, about the night. What if I flipped out again? What if he said the hell with it and left me alone out there . . . ?

I smoked a quarter pack of cigarettes before my shift ended.

When I got home, Jeffrey was at his post in front of the TV with some explosive video game. I didn't say anything as I walked by, consumed with deconstructing what had happened with David at work.

It didn't seem to bother Jeffrey that I'd ignored him, because no sooner had I gotten to my room than he barged straight in. In fairness, I hadn't closed the door yet.

"What's up?" Jeffrey said

"I'm going out to dinner with David Harowitz," I said, mostly to my carpet.

"David, the guy who drove me to Liam's?" Jeffrey asked excitedly. "Cool! Can I come?"

"Uh, no," I said. "Get out."

Jeffrey folded his arms. "No."

"Jeffrey . . ."

"You're so *bitchy* sometimes," Jeffrey declared.

I sat down on the edge of my bed so I'd be level with his eyes, then blinked as I realized he was already taller than me when I sat. I could've sworn just yesterday he came up to my stomach. He'd probably end up like our dad, tall with big hands and arms. When had he grown so much?

Had it really been that long since I'd paid attention?

"Only sometimes?" I said, and felt something like a grin disfiguring my face. "I must be improving."

Jeffrey tried to scowl but then laughed. Somehow I did too. Just a chuckle. Just a chortle or a snort. But it counted.

"How come you're going out at night?" Jeffrey said.

"I don't know. I just thought I'd give it a shot."

"It's been, like, forever."

"Yeah, I know, dude."

"That's cool."

Wow. Also, ouch.

"Thanks," I said.

I chased Jeffrey out and began getting ready. This took 6.3 millennia, because, honestly, I hadn't had to get ready for much of anything for a long time. My hands felt big and stupid as I sorted through clothes, trying to figure out what was appropriate. Then there was my rat's nest of a scalp. I scrambled through all of Mom's various brushes and combs. They may as well have been surgical instruments. What did this one do, what was that one for? Maybe I did need surgery.

So I had to risk moving to my next line of defense, not sure at all how it would play out.

"Mom?"

I found her in her bedroom, leaning against the headboard. The TV was on low, *Law & Order*—I'd seen it—and she held an e-reader in both hands.

Mom looked up. Her face was suspicious. "What?"

I almost turned right back around. Instead I lifted my chin and said, "What do you wear if it's not a date?"

The reader fell to her lap. "You have a date?"

"It's not a date," I said. "That's what I mean. We're just going to dinner."

"Who?"

The shock on her face didn't do much to calm my nerves. "David? From work?"

Mom's expression shifted. Slowly her eyebrows relaxed and a smile blossomed across her lips. "You're going out with him? When, tonight?"

"Mom . . ."

"You're going out," she went on. "At night."

"Mom, seriously, I don't—"

She flung herself out of bed like I'd announced she'd won the lottery. I wondered what I'd gotten myself into.

"Well let's just go see!" she said. She grabbed my arm and hustled me into my room. I hadn't seen her that excited since . . .

I don't know. It'd been a while.

"So when did this begin?" Mom asked, critically eyeing every shirt in my closet.

"Nothing began," I said, sitting on my bed. "I was just trying to apologize to him, and one thing led to another—"

Mom turned sharply.

"Not like that," I said.

"Apologize?" Mom said when her terror had passed. "For what?"

"I was just—he helped me out yesterday and I was a bitch about it, is all."

The sound of so much activity in my room roused Jeffrey, who poked his head through the doorway and said, "What're you *doing* in here?"

Mom and I both said, at the same time, "Girl stuff."

Snap. It wasn't my rubber band that time. It was my gut. Or maybe heart.

Jeffrey sneered and ran back to the living room. Mom laughed. A foreign sound. I almost did too. Except it was such a strong déjà vu moment, I couldn't. "Girl stuff" was how Tara and I always answered my dad, or hers, or even little Jeffrey when we didn't want to be bothered. Then we'd giggle hysterically.

"How about this?" Mom said, whirling around. She held up a crimson blouse and a pair of dark jeans. "Fun, sophisticated, but not too flirty . . . Jesus, is that a tag? Have you ever worn this, Pel? Doesn't matter, what do you think?"

I swallowed a cold lump of sudden sadness and nodded. Snapped my rubber band. "Sure," I said.

Mom changed her mind three times about my outfit. I'd been fine with the first, but she was enjoying herself so much, I couldn't stop her. Then she made me sit on the floor while she sat on the bed behind me and went to work on my hair.

We both were quiet while she worked. Mom used to do this all the time when I was little. This, like so many things, hadn't happened in a very long time.

Mom has magic hands when it comes to hair brushing. She puts me to sleep nearly every time. I couldn't believe I'd forgotten that.

"You know this *is* a date, right?" Mom said as she brushed.

"No, it's not."

"Penelope, when you ask a boy out to dinner, it's a date."

"It's not like that," I insisted. "He just . . . I don't know. Wants me to cheer up or something. So I'll be easier to work with."

"Well," Mom said, "just remember that when he's trying to get inside your shirt or worse."

"Mom! It's David. He's not like that."

"Honey, they're *all* like that."

From where I was sitting, her behind me, I couldn't tell if it was a joke or not. No big deal. I knew I was right.

When I stood up twenty minutes later and went to look in the bathroom mirror, my mouth dropped open. Mom slid beside me.

"Holy shit," I said.

Mom smirked. "I know, right?"

I was almost afraid to touch my hair. It hung straight and smooth, thick and full. I wasn't overly impressed with the color, which wasn't unusual for me, but—wow.

"Thank you," I said.

"You bet," Mom said. "Anytime. Does David smoke?"

Uh-oh. "No. I don't think so."

Mom put an arm around my shoulders, meeting my gaze

in our reflection. "Most people who don't, don't enjoy kissing people who do," she said. "Just a thought."

I met her eyes briefly in the mirror. Thought of all the little ways I believed she'd been out to get me, just like the world was out to get me. I guess the truth is, way down deep, I knew it wasn't true. Not about Mom, anyway. Probably I just confused the hell out of her, and she didn't know what to do. How to act. I mean, I didn't. Why should she be any different?

"Okay," I said to her.

She pulled me closer and kissed the side of my head. Then she went back to her room, leaving me to stare at my reflection.

I could leave my smokes at home, I guess. Not because David was going to kiss me, because he wasn't. But just to see if I could go the whole night. One small improvement, right?

Ten minutes later the doorbell rang. Jeffrey screamed that he'd get it, and ran full tilt to open the front door. I came walking behind him, and Mom trailing me, trying not to look like she was dying of curiosity.

David surprised me. He'd made an effort to look nice, it seemed, wearing a button-up short-sleeved shirt and nice jeans, and he'd swept his hair back a bit. It seemed like half his pimples had disappeared since work that afternoon.

"David!" Jeffrey shouted. "What's up, *man!*"

"Hey, dude," David said, raising his fist so Jeffrey could knuckle it. "How's it going?"

"I just beat the crap out of Fire Master," Jeffrey announced. "Wanna come see?"

"Oh, man, I'd love to, but we kinda need to get going," David said. "But maybe some other time we can team up and take on Time Master together. I've never beaten him."

"That would be awesome!" Jeffrey said.

"Hey," I said after Jeffrey ran back to his game.

"Hey," David said, smiling. Then his smile weakened. "You're looking at me funny."

"Oh. Sorry. No. I mean, I didn't mean to . . . you look good."

"Yeah? Cool. Thanks. You too."

"David, hello," Mom said, stepping beside me. "I'm Kris, Penelope's mom. How are you?"

"Good," David said, stretching out a hand. Mom shook it, looking impressed. "We won't be out late or anything."

Mom waved him off. "Oh, take your time," she said. "I'm just glad—"

Mom paused, took a breath, then finished, "Glad to get her out of my hair for a night." She rubbed my back in rough circles.

"Ready, then?" I said to David before Mom came any closer to being a total embarrassment.

"Yeah, let's go," David said. To Mom, he said, "Nice to meet you."

Mom said good-bye and followed us to the door. I felt her eyes on us the entire walk to his car.

"So, was that a thing?" David asked as we reached his car. "With your mom?"

"Sort of," I said.

"Are you, like, in trouble now? Because I don't want you to—"

"Nope," I said. "Everything's fine. Where did you say we were going?"

NINE

We didn't talk much on the drive. I kept folding and refolding my hands in my lap, chewing my lips raw, hating that I'd left my smokes at home, wondering when the next big meltdown was going to arrive.

Yet somehow I made it to the restaurant without getting kidnapped or killed. For once, I felt my heartbeat slow down a bit. It still raced along; I still kept swiveling my head in every possible direction to look for threats; my stomach still rolled and jolted.

But I was *here*.

David guided us into Orange Table, where I ordered a dinner sandwich and Italian soda. David, sure enough, got his enormous hamburger. I had to admit, it did sound pretty tasty. The small restaurant reminded me of the Hole in the Wall in that it wasn't one link in a long chain of look-alike restaurants. But it was also more upscale than the Hole ever could or would be. Or probably even wanted to be. A woman kept rushing around to all the tables, saying hellos, making sure everything was good. She had this bright orange-dyed hair that would've seemed out of place anywhere else. Here she became part of the décor. Her hair matched the color of all the tabletops.

David and I chatted lightly about work for the most part. It was easy enough. But I could feel weight underneath. Like we were skimming the surface when there was more to be had if we'd just dive down. When our food arrived, it took only a couple of minutes to notice neither one of us was eating very earnestly. David seemed nervous. Or maybe bored. Hard to tell. Either way, I wished he'd eat more so I could at least tell myself I'd paid him back.

As his burger cooled and my sandwich warmed, David cleared his throat and said, "So, um . . . I hate to ask the obvious, but are you absolutely a hundred percent sure it was Tara the other day?"

Good thing I already didn't have an appetite.

"Why would you ask me that?" I said.

David said, "Because for some stupid reason, I still want to help. I mean, if you want."

"Help *how*?" I pushed my plate away. "I've gotten all the professional help I could ever use."

David raised an eyebrow.

Great job, Pelly, I thought. *Why don't you just hand over your medical file while you're at it, so he can see how stupid he is for wanting to help out the local nut factory?*

"Never mind," I said. I took a sip of my vanilla soda. Which was incredibly tasty, with thick cream poured in it and everything. But it didn't help.

So we sat for a while, with David shifting in his seat every other minute. I sat with my shoulders rolled forward, trying to tuck my chin into my throat.

"So," David said. "This is . . . fun."

"Yeah," I said helplessly. "That's me. Tons of fun."

"Your hair looks, um, nice," he said.

"Thanks."

"I don't think I've ever seen it . . . you know . . ."

"Brushed?"

"I was trying to say styled, but. Okay."

David finally took another bite of his burger. His eyes widened for a moment. "So that's still the best burger ever," he muttered. But didn't take another bite.

"So in a weird reversal," I said, "it's my turn to ask you. Are *you* okay?"

"Yeah. Tip-top. You?"

"Mm-hmm."

"Good. That's . . . good." He paused, then spoke to the tabletop. He said, very quietly, "This isn't working."

"I'm sorry—" I began to say, but he cut me off.

"No, it's me, I shouldn't have made you do this."

"I asked you."

"Yeah, but you didn't mean, as in, like . . . like a . . ."

"Like a date?" I whispered.

"Yes. Yes, like a date. That's not what you meant." David lifted his eyes. "Is it?"

"No," I said quickly, so he wouldn't be mad. Or grossed out. "No, I just really wanted to say thanks and apologize and all that."

His eyes lowered again. "Right," he said.

Unexpectedly I heard Mom's voice echoing in my head. How she insisted this was, in fact, a date. That hadn't been my intent at the Hole in the Wall, when I asked him. But it was one thing for David to misconstrue it. It was another for him to have wanted it.

So in a stutter I asked, "Did—you—want it? To be? A date?"

David didn't answer right away.

"Thing is," he said finally, "yeah. Kind of. I mean, you're so . . . you're just . . ."

Then he sighed. "Okay, the hell with it. You're cute. Okay? You're cute, I said it. I think you're cute. You are so . . . fuck-ing . . . cute. But at work you're just—you're always so . . ."

"Bitchy." I didn't look at him. Couldn't. I knew what was what. And besides—

Cute? Whatever. Not in this lifetime.

Right?

"Yes!" David said, like it was relief. I had to shake my head to focus back on what he was saying. "Yes, bitchy! Thank God, yes. Yes. Sorry. I don't mean to drive it home or anything, but

God, yes. Bitchy or just ice queen, and there were so many times I thought about asking you out or something, but when I got up the guts, you'd have this evil glare or whatever, so I never did."

"Oh," I said softly.

"But then sometimes," David said, *his* voice also softening, "I'd catch you just sort of staring off, and your face wasn't all tight. I always wondered what you were thinking about, because you'd look so relaxed. But it never lasted. As soon as someone walked in, or I said something, you'd tighten back up again."

I didn't want to believe I knew what he was talking about, but I did. I knew exactly. Those times I looked relaxed must've been the times I let myself think about what life would be like if I was normal. If I could go places like a regular person. Go on dates, for instance. Or school.

How many kids actually dream about that? Probably just the ones who can't.

In any case, I had pressing matters to attend to here.

"Could you back up a bit?" I said. "To the whole 'cute' part? Because I have to ask, are you serious?"

David met my eyes. Held them. Nodded after a moment.

"Yeah," he said.

And that was all for a minute. We sat there silently until David thumped his fingers on the table and said, "So, there, it's out, no taking it back. If you don't feel the same way, and honestly, I don't think you do, then . . . okay. Cool. I can handle it, and I won't be a creeper about it. I'll even quit the Hole if it bothers you. I don't actually need the money all that bad, I was kidding about that yesterday . . . but honestly, Pel, this kidnapping thing, that must've been a huge deal, right? I'm sorry if I'm prying, and you can tell me to back off right now, and we'll talk about something easy like the weather, or politics and religion, whatever. But I want to know everything. I do. That's it. Glutton for punishment, I guess."

He took a deep breath and chased the words down with a long drink from his raspberry Italian soda.

I sat still, arms stiff at my sides, gripping my chair seat in sweaty fingers.

"Could you repeat that?" I said.

David hesitated, then burst into laughter.

And I . . . smiled. It was the last thing I expected to do, trust me, but it happened all the same.

I reached out and took a bite of my sandwich as my appetite came roaring back. I don't know if it was just the food or not, but it tasted fantastic.

I took my time chewing the huge bite while David fiddled with his drink. I wondered if he was sweating as much as the glass. It wasn't as if I hadn't *ever* kind of considered how he felt about me. I'm not a complete social idiot. Not completely. But what he said wasn't what I'd expected. Now that it was out, I sort of waited to feel awkward or embarrassed for him.

I didn't.

I felt . . . sorta good.

"Pelly?"

"Huh?"

"You haven't said anything for twenty minutes."

"Are you serious?" I said. It wouldn't have surprised me.

"No," David said. "It's probably been, like, thirty seconds. I'm just really impatient."

I felt myself smiling again, and he smiled back. It wasn't forced, either.

I folded my arms on the table and pressed myself against its edge, leaning toward him. "Pardon my French," I said, "but you have to understand that I'm really well and truly fucked up in the head."

David imitated my stance, leaning closer. "Wow," he whispered. "And you're the *only one* on the planet. Incredible."

"I should slap you."

"But it might turn me on, and then what?"

I groaned. "Are you like this at work and I just never noticed?"

David sat back. "Not as much, no," he said. "My friend Mark's parents own this place. I've been coming here since we were little. It's kind of a home-turf-advantage thing."

"Ah," I said. I stalled by taking another bite. So David did too. I looked at the art on the walls. Listened to the low buzz of conversation, the shouted orders to the cook in the back. The woman with the orange hair gave David what would have been an expert clandestine motherly wink if I hadn't happened to be glancing that way. The whole place was enough like the

Hole to make me feel more at home, even if it was David's turf. Even if it was nighttime . . .

My heart cut left, then right, then down, then up. Like a racquetball pinging off my ribs. It was night, nighttime, it was dark out, and—

I drew in a breath. Held it. Stopped intrusive thoughts. Exhaled. Knew what I had to say next as David watched me do all that with a curious expression.

"I'm not sure how I'm supposed to say what I need to say here," I said, staring in his direction but not at him directly. "So I'm just going to kind of blather and see what happens?"

"Perfect," David said. "I'll eat, you blather."

"Okay," I said. "It's like this. This one morning about a month after Tara was taken, I got ready for school just like always, but then I couldn't leave the house. I physically could not step out the door. Mom let me stay home that day, but not the next, and I—I mean, I just lost it. The bus ride, my first class, I was wrecked. I wasn't even crying, I just couldn't stop shaking and I felt sick to my stomach."

David nodded, his eyes never leaving my face. "Like the other day at work? When you said someone had been staring at you?"

"Pretty much, yeah," I said. I felt absurdly guilty for it. "And it's been that way ever since, more or less. My parents put me into therapy, which I guess worked, eventually. My doctor put me on meds, and I was able to at least go outside again after a while. But not at night. And I didn't like how the meds made me feel. Sort of slow and loopy, you know? It's like, everything is okay when I'm on them, but *only* okay. Never good, or great. Just okay."

"Isn't that the point? I mean, it's a bummer, I get that, but I thought that kind of medication was *supposed* to make everything just okay."

"Maybe, but it sucks. It's like, hey, you just won a million dollars! *Okay.* Oh no, your kitten got hit by a tractor trailer! *Okay.* Everything's level. Which I guess is nice, because there's no real lows. Not as much panic or anger. But no highs, either. No joy. You know?"

David gave a little sound, and nodded. I found myself wanting to stop there. Cut my losses. Instead I kept talking. Maybe it was *because* I wasn't on my meds anymore.

"The truth is, I'm scared. My dad's never home, my mom works all the time, and Jeffrey . . . it's like everyone I love is going to leave, or be taken away, and I just can't do that again. What if my dad's plane goes down, what if someone attacks my mom or takes . . . I can't go through it. Can't risk it. I don't even like talking to my own little brother because if something happened to him, too . . ."

A faraway part of my mind realized that David had put a hand on top of mine. I looked at our hands there on the orange tabletop and stared blankly. David blinked and pulled his hand away.

"Sorry," he said.

"No, no, it's okay, it's no big deal—"

"About what you've been through, I mean," David said. "That's what I'm sorry about."

". . . Oh."

David finished off his burger. I picked at my sandwich. When he was done, he wiped his hands and mouth with his napkin and asked, "So, then, what about Tara?"

"What about her?"

"What do you want to do?" His hazel eyes were more serious than I'd ever seen them.

"What *can* I do? They'll find her, or they won't. Probably won't. And I'll get over it."

I almost added *again*.

"You sure?" David asked.

"Yes," I said, though I wasn't. "I mean, maybe I'm a little 'detached,' as my therapist says. Maybe that's a good thing."

"You don't really believe that, do you?"

"Sometimes. Yeah. A lot."

"That must suck," David said.

For some reason, the simplicity of his statement had never dawned on me. "You're right," I said, half to myself. "It kind of does. Fortunately, I've got my insanity to keep me company."

"I don't think you're insane."

"The voices in my head beg to differ."

"You hear voices, huh?"

"Not voices, plural. And no, not . . . voices, just . . ." I scrambled for a definition. "Don't you ever feel like there's someone in your head telling you that you'll never be good enough, or that you're really all alone, or that you suck, or you're ugly, or a failure. Things like that?"

David's expression dropped. "Absolutely," he said. "Everyone does. Anyone who says they don't is a liar."

"Right," I said. "Well, mine tells me I'm . . . that it's my fault. That it's a curse. That everyone I love will get hurt or go away."

"I get it," David said. "Gotcha. So not, like, schizophrenic . . ."

"No, not schizophrenic. And you're confusing that with multiple personalities. I don't have that. Either one, I mean."

David shrugged. "I think there's a case to be made that we *all* have multiple personalities, but I see your point. Regardless, I don't think that particular voice makes you insane."

"What does it make me?"

David's lips twisted around on his face for a moment as he thought. "To put it lightly?" he said. "Bummed out. It makes you majorly bummed out."

"Okay," I said. "That's fair."

"So what can I do?" David asked. "I want to help, Pelly. I mean, regardless of where we—of how you . . . you know."

I thought back to the creepy guy's license plate, and the website I'd saved to my favorites. Wondered if maybe David had a credit card.

And snapped my rubber band.

It wouldn't be fair. He'd just told me he liked me, and while his sincerity seemed genuine, I couldn't just start using him for his money, for God's sake. Maybe I was insane, but I was not a freaking gold digger.

"Nothing," I said. "Nothing at all. Except maybe change the subject."

"Okay. You watch *Saturday Night Live*?"

And with that, we stuck to talking about TV, movies, and music for the most part, although I did tell him some of Jeffrey's more embarrassing stories from when he was little. So that was fun.

"Are you sure you can afford all that?" he asked as we walked out of the restaurant.

"Sure," I said. "I don't know what Eli pays you, but I'm in the upper six figures now."

David laughed, and something I barely recognized as one came out of my mouth.

"What else do you like to do, anyway?" David asked.

"I'm not really sure," I said, trying to hide my embarrassment. "Getting the job at the Hole in the Wall was kind of a test. See if I could be out and productive. I still don't get out much."

Truer words were never spoken. Apart from school and dinner, I mostly watched movies or read. Sometimes both at the same time. Jeffrey might've had an incurable video game addiction, but we were both still big readers. Mom and Dad were definitely a part of that. Between the four of us, our combined household library sustained me for six years.

"Don't get out much," David said thoughtfully. Then he asked, "What do you want to try?"

"School," I said.

"Ha, wow. That'd be quite a hot night out. You party animal."

"No, I know, it's weird. I do online school. Which is okay. Maybe I'd actually hate being on a campus, but since I haven't been in so long, I don't really know. I guess it's more that I'd like to be *able* to do it. Whether I liked it or not is sort of irrelevant."

David considered my logic. "I guess it's one of those 'don't know what you got till it's gone' type things, huh?"

"Yeah. Something like that."

"That's cool," David said. "But what about going-out type stuff? You want to try movies, or dancing, or—I don't know, hang gliding?"

"Those would all be great if I could get out of my house."

"Pelly?"

"Hmm."

"You're out of your house right now, I'm not sure if you realize that."

I think I smiled.

"Well, if you ever want, I know an after-hours club that's pretty cool," he said, and started doing a little tap dance in his sneakers as we walked. "I'll have to show you my moves."

"You dance, too? What happened to martial arts?"

"My mom thought I needed to be kept busy, I guess. She's right."

"You know tap?"

"A smidgen. Maybe a pinch."

"Cool," I said.

David began whistling. I'd never heard him do that before;

I mean, really, who walks around whistling? But it was kinda cute. And he was oddly good at it.

Then he put both hands in his pockets and did this dance-step thing, like a skip and a jump, which made me smile. He smiled right back and shrugged happily.

"A fighter and a dancer," I said.

"And a black-belt barista," David said. He grinned and started up his little jig again.

Then he jingled his keys in his pocket. *Jang, jang, jang.*

"So," he said, "you want to get ice cream or—"

"Stop!" I shouted at him, so loud it brought me to a halt.

David froze, eyes flying open. "What—"

He'd silenced the keys. But I could hear them ringing in my ears, *jang, jang, jang . . .*

"Stop!" I cried again, my hands hovering in front of me as I fought the urge to cover my ears.

"Pelly? What is it?"

Jang, jang, jang . . .

Him.

He was there.

"God, what—" My eyes started to pinwheel. "I . . . oh my God . . ."

David held out his arms, as if to catch me. "Pelly, what is it? Your face, you're all white."

Jang, jang, jang . . .

He was there and he followed us, oh God, he'd been following us, stalking us, picking us out—

I reached for David's arm, clutched it, and let myself sit down on the blacktop, right in the middle of the parking lot. David followed me down, looking into my eyes.

"Tell me what to do," he said, firm and calm. "Should I call for help?"

I worked for a long moment to try to get spit into my mouth. It had gone as dry as a grave.

"He was there," I whispered finally. I could not generate any spit. "In the store. Watching us."

"Who was where, Pelly?"

"The man who came into the Hole in the Wall. With Tara. Wednesday. It was him."

I don't think I'd blinked in the last two full minutes.

"He was in the store the day she disappeared. Jingling his keys. David, that was him!"

TEN

Every muscle in my body went rigid and locked in place as David drove us back to my house. All thoughts of David's confession of devotion, or whatever it had been, were gone. All I could feel—all I could *taste*—was the sound of those keys jingling in that sick old man's pocket. *Jang, jang, jang* . . .

"You should take a breath at some point," David said.

"Huh?" I gasped.

"Breathe," David said softly. "Take deep breaths. Four counts in, six counts out. C'mon."

"I can't."

"Yes, you can."

I didn't know whether to punch him or hug him. I split the difference and tried his technique instead. Much as I hate to admit it, by the time we rolled up to the sidewalk in front of my house, I did feel slightly more relaxed.

That didn't stop me from leaping out of the car at top speed and racing for the front door. I don't know if I was surprised or not when David appeared at my shoulder. And I didn't care. I had things to do.

I threw open the door and rushed in, barely registering Mom and Jeffrey on the couch watching a movie. Mom practically jumped up from the couch as I ran past.

"Penelope!" she said. "What on earth—"

"Not now," I said, beelining for my bedroom.

I got inside. Flipped the light. Got my laptop fired up before David and Mom showed up together at my doorway.

"You're home early," Mom remarked. She might've glared mildly at David. Suspicious. Maybe imagining that whole get-inside-your-shirt thing.

"I don't have time," I said, already facing my laptop screen and bringing up the license plate website.

Mom turned to David. "Is everything all right?"

"Uh . . ." David looked at me.

"No, it's not all right!" I said. "I mean—yes, David is fine, we're fine, I just remembered something and I have to look this thing up real quick and I just . . . need quiet!"

Mom gave up, moving back down the hall. David tentatively stuck his face past the threshold.

"Should I go?" he asked.

Impatiently I waved him inside. "Shut the door."

He did it. Took a seat on the floor, resting his back against the foot of my bed. "What're you doing?"

I filled in the information on the website, then swiveled my chair toward David. "Listen," I said, "I have to ask you a favor, and I absolutely need you to say no if you don't want to do it."

I could see his shields going up again. "Okay . . . "

"Do you have a credit card or anything like that?"

For the first time ever, I saw David's face become suspicious. "Debit card, yeah," he said. "My dad wanted me to have it to learn how to budget or whatever, since no one uses cash anymore."

"I need it. Need to use it, I mean."

"What for?" he asked, but his hand drifted toward his pocket.

I rolled away from the desk so he could see the screen. "I can use this website to look up that guy's license plate," I said. "Find out where he lives, criminal record, everything."

David had his wallet out by then but held it closed. "Is that the best idea?"

"It's the only idea I have left," I said. "David, no one is going to believe me about the keys. I don't know if I picked out the right guy in that photo lineup. Tara's parents hate me. This is all I got."

"I don't think they hate you."

"Doesn't matter," I said. "I need to do this. Look, I've got the cash to pay you back right here if that's what—"

"It's not." David tapped his wallet against his other hand. "What're you going to do once you have the information?"

Huh. That was a good point.

"I don't know," I admitted. "But once I have it, maybe I'll come up with something. Seeing the information might, you know. Trigger an idea."

David didn't look convinced. He studied me closely for a minute, then pulled a card out of his wallet and handed it to me. "Okay," he said. "I trust you."

When he said that, I felt the corners of my eyes pinch. I cleared my throat and said thanks, then put his info into the site. A minute later I had everything I needed.

"Franklin Rebane," I reported to David.

He'd been reading the spines of all my books. When I spoke, he got up and leaned over to read the screen with me.

"Canyon City," David said. "That's, what, two hours from here?"

"Round about," I said. "No criminal record. Damn it."

"You were hoping?"

"I was *assuming*. And then if he did have one, it would make the cops take more interest, maybe."

"So since he doesn't have any kind of record," David said, "doesn't that sort of at least *suggest* he's not a—"

"Look," I said, standing up and pacing around my room as David took my chair and continued scrolling through Rebane's information. "Here's the facts. I saw my best friend at the Hole in the Wall with someone driving Franklin Rebane's car. That's not up for debate. Maybe the man she was with isn't this Rebane guy, maybe he stole the car, maybe he borrowed it. Who knows. But that's the first step. That's it. I have to see if the guy driving that car is Rebane or not, and then go from there."

"I don't get it," David said, twisting back and forth in my chair. "What's that going to prove?"

"If the creepy old guy from the Hole isn't Rebane, then Rebane may know who he is," I said. "If that wasn't him, then the cops might be looking for the wrong guy."

"And if it was him?"

"If it was him . . . then I need to know more."

"Okay," David said, "so how do you plan on doing that?"

I folded my arms and raised my eyebrows hopefully. "You want to take me on a road trip to Canyon City tomorrow?"

ELEVEN

The next day, my insides jiggled as I waited in the kitchen for David to arrive. Whether it was because we were about to track down a kidnapper, or just because we would be alone together all afternoon, I didn't know.

"Arncha gonna have lunch?" Jeffrey demanded as he smeared an inch of strawberry jam on a piece of white bread.

"Not hungry," I grumbled.

"You're being bitchy again," Jeffrey said.

"Imagine that."

"Yep. Me and Mom are gonna go see a movie today, and I was gonna ask you, but now you can't come, I don't care what you say."

"No kidding?" I asked. "I mean, Mom's really taking you to the movies?" Usually she worked all day.

"Yep."

"That's awesome," I told him. "Seriously."

"I know," Jeffrey said. "You still can't come, though."

"I have plans, dude," I said, and my nerves buzzed again.

"With *Day*-vid?" Jeffrey said, acting like a little kid.

"He's driving me, yeah," I said. "Don't say it like that."

Jeffrey grinned, and I could see the teenager he was so close to becoming. Very weird.

At six minutes past noon David drove up in his red pickup. My nerves did their electric shock thing again.

"Gotta go," I said to my brother. "Tell Mom I won't be home till late."

"You're gonna get in trouble," Jeffrey said, delighting in the idea.

"Yeah, well, don't hold your breath," I said. I hadn't been in any trouble since—well, ever. Not in the last six years, anyway.

"I like your hair," Jeffrey called as I opened our front door.

I paused. "What?"

"Your hair," Jeffrey said. "It's all, like, straight and stuff."

I hadn't noticed. I must've brushed it out after my shower. Or maybe I just didn't want to know that I'd done it.

"Well, um . . . thanks," I said.

He waved. I went outside. Patted all my pockets to make sure I had everything: smokes, lighter, band around my wrist, pillbox, shoulder bag with wallet, phone, tissues, snack, water. Good to go. If the apocalypse began, I'd be ready.

I met David halfway up our walk. He wore jeans, sneakers, and a white thermal beneath a black T-shirt. He'd done something more with his hair again, different even from last night. And it looked good. I tried to tell myself he didn't do it for me, because to assume that would be so freaking arrogant. Except . . . after what he had said last night, was it really so wrong to believe that?

"Howdy," David said.

I tripped on my sidewalk with a grunt.

"Uh—hi," I said. Nice start to the day.

"You want to get something to eat on the way?" David asked as we walked to the truck.

"Sure," I blurted, even though I still wasn't hungry.

"Cool," David said as we climbed in. "We'll stop by the Hole. I think Harriet's working. She'll hook us up."

I almost choked at the double entendre. Since David didn't seem to notice he'd said it, I just looked out the window.

"I'll cover gas," I said.

"No worries," David said. "I got it."

"David, no, seriously."

"Penelope, yes, seriously," David said. He said my name with the wrong emphasis: PENNEL-ope. It was stupid. And I liked it.

"But it's my mission," I said.

"And I'm a mission support specialist," David said. "I'll do my job, you do yours. That's how it works."

"Why are you doing this?"

I felt him glance at me. "I told you I wanted to help."

"Yeah, but why?"

David laughed, but nervously. "Thought I pretty much covered that last night."

"Really?" I turned to face him. "I mean, that's *really* the reason."

David opened his eyes real wide and tried to start about a dozen sentences. Finally he said, "Honestly? It's most of the reason, yeah. But, um . . . look, maybe I shouldn't go into this right now, big mission coming up and everything."

"What? Tell me."

"I think you're wrong."

Panic attacks feel like heart attacks. This felt like a punch in the stomach.

"About *what*?" My voice squeaked.

David looked worried. Also, determined. We turned onto McDowell, headed toward the café.

"About Tara," he said. "I think maybe you saw someone who looked like her. And maybe, sure, the guy you saw jingled his keys. Lots of people do that. Obviously. I mean, I did it, but that doesn't make me a kidnapper. Didn't seem like her mom was on board. I'm sure that detective is going to look into it, like he said he would, and . . . I don't know. I'm happy to do this for you, regardless, but a big part of it, Pelly, a huge freaking part of it is to show you that nothing strange has happened, that you didn't see your friend, but that maybe you *needed* to. And the sooner you see it wasn't her, the sooner you'll feel better."

He paused.

"And that's what I really want," he said. "The you-feeling-better part."

I watched him in silence while he kept driving. I must've made him uncomfortable, because after a while he kept shifting in his seat. But he didn't say anything.

He had a point.

I knew that. I was insane, but not necessarily stupid. I did need to find Tara. If I could do that, I could undo all the stupid things that had gone on since she had disappeared. I could get my life back together. Be normal. Go places. Go on dates. Things like that. And if, somehow, I was totally wrong and the girl from the café wasn't her . . . at least I'd done something.

"You're right," I said quietly, turning to face front again. "Maybe it wasn't Tara I saw. But I have to know for sure. This is the first time I've done something. Like, taken action. You know? I have to see for myself. That's all."

"You're wrong about that, too."

"Wow," I said. "This whole 'bold you' thing? It's got a kick at the end."

"This isn't the first time you've taken action, you got the job at the Hole," David said, unfazed. "You went out last night. How easy was that?"

"Not very," I mumbled.

"Right. So this . . . I mean, this is a big deal. I think. Don't sell yourself short."

I wanted to say something snarky-like. But I didn't.

"Anyway," David said. "I got your back the whole way."

"Thank you," I said as we pulled into the dirt parking lot of the Hole in the Wall.

David turned to look into my eyes. "Anytime."

Neither of us was scheduled this particular Saturday. As we went to the counter and placed our orders with Harriet—who looked very confused both at two employees ordering hot chocolate and sweet rolls for lunch, and that those two employees were us—I began wondering who David and I were now.

I mean, I'd been on dates. Sort of. Group things with people from my day treatment group therapy program, for the most part. There'd been a fun little Greek restaurant nearby, and in broad daylight, surrounded by people like Alecia, I'd felt mostly safe. I'd had a couple of awkward, clandestine kisses here and there with a guy from "Groop," which I really do not care to get into. But that's it.

Last night at Orange Table with David, what did that make us? Were we boyfriend/girlfriend? Something else? Same as always? Friends with benefits, that kind of thing? It's not like we'd kissed. He'd told me how he felt, and that was it. I hadn't even told him how *I* felt.

Probably because I didn't know. This was all new. Unexpected. As if seeing Tara wasn't enough to throw my world into a new orbit, now there was David.

I almost dropped my hot chocolate when Harriet handed it to me. David didn't say anything as we walked back out to the car with Harriet eyeing us the whole way. I wondered if there was a rule against coworkers dating. Or if maybe Harriet liked David. Or if maybe David actually liked Harriet, and he was just using me somehow to get to her. . . .

"There's smoke coming out of your ears," David said.

I bumped into the truck. "Huh?"

"You're thinking way too hard," David said. "What's up? Is it the cocoa? Because I bet I can have Harriet fired. I have that kind of pull."

"Sorry, no," I said, bypassing his joke. "I mean, I'm fine."

"Okay," David said. "You ready to do this?"

I nodded.

"Are you positive you *want* to?" he asked.

"No."

David looked as surprised as I felt. He opened his mouth, but I cut him off.

"I just mean, like you said, I could be wrong about this whole thing. All of it. And what happens then?"

"Then we come home," David said. "That's all."

"Yeah, we come home, but then what for me?" I said. "If I can't get Tara back, then . . ."

David said nothing, only waited for me.

"Then maybe nothing will ever change," I went on.

"Well," David said slowly, "let's find out. C'mon."

He climbed into the driver's seat. I stood outside the passenger door for another moment, staring blankly at the empty space his body had just occupied.

"Okay," I whispered to his ghost, and got in.

David was a very safe driver for seventeen. Or maybe he was a very safe driver *because* he was seventeen, I couldn't tell. He got us onto the freeway that would connect to the highway out of town, nice and smooth. Of course, on an early Saturday morning there wasn't much traffic to contend with, which helped.

I couldn't get my mind to settle down on any one topic. Thoughts ricocheted from one side of my skull to the other until I could barely keep my eyes open.

"What's your family like?" I asked, trying to get something to focus on.

"Pretty decent," David said. "For family."

"What do they do?"

"My mom's an editor for a health magazine," David said. "Like, for vitamins and stuff. And my dad's a dealer."

Well, that certainly got me to think about something new.

"*Drugs?*" I said.

"Blackjack."

"What's blackjack? Is that some kind of heroin or something?"

David laughed out loud. I thought for a second he'd run us off the road, careful driver or not. "Blackjack, the card game," he said. "He works at one of the casinos on the reservation."

"Oh," I said, and sat back in my seat. "God. I thought . . . wait a sec, you did that on purpose, didn't you."

David gave me a theatrical, innocent shrug.

And I smiled. "Can I smoke in here?"

"Nope."

"Oh. Okay."

"It's hard to get the smell out. You know."

"Sure, yeah. It's okay."

"Do you want me to pull over? We can park, take a break."

"We've been on the road for, like, ten minutes."

"Yes, but see, I'm flexible that way."

"I can make it," I said, looking out my window. "I shouldn't do it anyway."

"Why do you?" he asked.

I bit my lip, reconsidering his offer to pull over. Damn. Once the desire was in my head, it wouldn't go away. So much for not being addicted. Or self-medicating. That's what Dr. Carpenter called it.

"Okay, pull over," I said. "I mean, when you get a chance."

"How about once we hit the 17?"

"Okay."

David kept an eye out. About fifteen minutes later, outside of Phoenix proper, he found a big stretch of dirt and slowed. He pulled off, and we climbed out together. We stood on either side of the bed of the truck, draping our forearms over the sides, facing each other. Traffic zoomed past, uncaring. I wondered what they thought of us. Of who—or what—we were.

I lit my cigarette and tilted my head back, blowing the smoke up. Wind frittered it away into nothing. It was getting chilly.

"It's going to be cold up there," I said, avoiding his eyes.

"I've got an extra sweatshirt behind the seat if you need it."

"Not yet, but thanks." I took another drag and shut my mouth, blowing the smoke out of my nose. "I picked it up a couple years ago," I said finally. "From some—people. I was going to say friends, but they weren't, really. Just people I knew."

"Those darn kids from the wrong side of the tracks?" David asked. "Getting you involved with the wrong sorts of people? What with their long hair and disregard for authority."

"No. Nothing like that. It was just around, and I picked it up. It was something to do."

"You should give it up."

"I know."

"I mean, when you're ready."

"Yeah."

"I personally don't care," David said. "But I think you'd be happier without them."

"Happier," I mumbled, blowing out a cloud.

"Someone buys them for you, you said?"

"Yeah, I got a guy. Well, a girl. But she always says that about stuff. Whatever you need done, she's 'got a guy' who can do it."

"So she's a friend."

I stamped the cigarette out in the dirt. "Not exactly," I said. "She isn't *not*, I guess. Met her at my doctor's office. She buys them for me once a week."

"I don't know if you know this, but you sound like you don't like her very much."

I pulled out another smoke. Lit it. Kept it between my lips as I answered, giving me that unique smoker's lisp. "What d'you shink?"

"I think there's a lot you don't talk about."

I froze in place, eyeing him through gray smoke. David gazed easily back at me, his face friendly. I pulled the smoke out with my fingers. Stood there looking at David carefully.

A brand-new thought came to mind. Something I'd never considered. Something Dr. Carpenter had never suggested. Something that made me feel both really guilty and at least a little excited.

In the *Wizard of Oz* movie, when Dorothy is in Kansas, everything's in black and white. In Oz it's in full color. As I was standing across from David at that moment, his image went from black and white to color. Like I'd never really seen him fully for who he was till that moment.

I'm not saying I was in love with him. How could someone say that with any certainty in this situation? Even *he* hadn't said that. I'm not saying I suddenly wanted to throw him into bed or something. Thanks to my meds these past years, I barely had an inkling of what being "turned on" even felt like. I'm only saying that he seemed different. And that maybe following him into Oz for a little while just might work out.

I crushed my cigarette out on the ground, only half-smoked. "Let's go," I said.

David slapped a palm against the edge of the truck bed

with a metallic thud. "You got it," he said. A minute later we were back on the road.

It didn't take long for me to realize I was able to relax and have an actual conversation with David. Not that we solved the mysteries of the universe or anything, but we just—you know. Hung out. Like a real road trip. And when I started veering into worry and panic, I snapped my rubber band and reminded myself there'd be plenty of time for both when we got to Canyon City.

David insisted on pumping the gas when we stopped at a place called Cordes, a truck stop about halfway to Canyon City. I didn't want him to do the work himself. But once he wrestled the nozzle away from me, I didn't mind so much. I hopped onto the hood and banged my heels against one tire while he worked.

"I'll pay," I said.

"No, I got it," David said.

"I know how much you make, remember," I said, shivering in a sudden breeze. It was cooler up here. I wished I'd brought more than my thin jacket. I wondered how much colder it would be in Canyon City.

"It's okay, really," David said. "I'm covered."

"Are you, like, independently wealthy or something?"

"No . . . but my sifu pays me a bit to teach the little kids sometimes," David said.

"What's a see-foo?"

"My wing chun teacher."

"You teach little kids to kick ass, huh?"

"Not quite," David answered. "It's not about kicking ass. It's about . . . peace."

"Peace through punching."

"Peace through blending, remember?" he said. "Blend with your opponents instead of trying to match or beat their strength. Then it doesn't matter how much bigger or stronger he is."

"I wish I could believe that," I said.

"I'll teach you," David said.

Only this time he didn't try to apologize for it. I'd never seen this kind of confidence from him before. It was relaxing somehow. I didn't fight a small smile.

David caught me doing it and laughed. "See, now, is it so bad to be in a good mood once in a while?"

"Sorry," I said.

David stood beside me, leaning against the side of the truck. "Hey," he said softly. "I wasn't trying to be a jerk. I just like seeing you happy for a change. Can't you feel the difference?"

I frowned. "I guess."

"But you're not really digging it."

"It's new," I admitted.

I tilted my head to the clear sky above us. Such a beautiful part of the state. I hoped Tara was outside enjoying it. Behind and below us, the "Valley of the Sun" lay bland and familiar as the smudged pink walls of my room. Up here, rounded granite boulders reflected almost red, dotted with narrow green bushes.

"Can I tell you something?" I said.

"I sure hope so."

"I spent some time in a . . . hospital," I said.

"Appendix? Hangnail?"

"Not exactly. It was a—you know. Like, mental hospital." It came out *mennel hospil*, I said it so fast.

David blinked a couple times. Sucked in a breath through his nose. Nodded.

"Okay."

I glared at him through slitted eyes. "You don't think that's weird?"

David shrugged. "Maybe. Or not weird so much as, like, rare. Unusual. I mean, come on, Pel. Your best friend got kidnapped. I think you earned a little mental health break."

"It doesn't freak you out?"

"I can say yes if that'll make you feel better," David said. "It doesn't happen to everyone, no, so it's weird like that. And I mean, it's—well, if you're sick, you go get help. At a hospital. Doesn't matter what kind of sick or what kind of hospital. *Are* you sick?"

"Sure feels that way."

"Are you, like, going to hurt yourself? Because I swear to God, you try any shit like that, I'll drive you right back to that hospital myself."

I thought about my legs. What he might think if I showed

them. Then I processed his threat. How could a threat make me feel good? Very strange.

"No," I said. It was true at the moment, anyway. I wanted a cigarette more than my cutting blade. Still, my fingers drifted to the pillbox just to make sure it was still there.

"That's good," David said. "So, then, no big deal."

I didn't respond. Not right away. The gas was done pumping by then. He put the handle back, snapped the gas cap lid closed, and leaned against the car. Beside me.

"I was only there a few days," I said at last. "Well, and then day treatment after that. But what I wanted to say about it . . . what I wanted to tell you . . ."

It was actually harder to admit to this part. David crossed his arms over his chest, not saying a word. Just waiting. I loved that he did that.

I gazed across the highway, watching the rare car drive by. Another breeze dimpled the skin on my arms. I wished we were just on a regular road trip.

"It's easier," I said finally, saying the words I'd never even said to myself but knew were true. "They do everything. It's almost like a vacation, except for the therapy and the meds and the blood tests every morning."

David winced.

"Yeah," I said. "Like freaking vampires, I swear. But still. It was easier. No one really expects anything from you. If you want to be alone, you just whip up a fresh batch of tears, get a pass to go back to your room. The food wasn't great, but it didn't suck. You don't even have to do homework necessarily. You're this fragile little bird and everyone bends over backward to make sure you don't get upset. It's kind of a sweet deal. *That's* where I picked up smoking. There's this patio outside the living area, with a lighter bolted to the wall, kind of like a cigarette lighter in a car. We couldn't have our own lighters. No lighters, no matches. No sharps. No shoelaces. Some of them couldn't even have pencils."

"Did you try to . . . you know."

I knew.

"No," I said. "But I'm not sure why not, really."

David squinted at me.

"I just mean—" I hesitated, not sure how to describe it. "Are you claustrophobic at all?"

"Not especially," he said. "I did get stuck on a roller coaster once. That was pretty terrifying. So we were out in the open and everything, but it took hours for them to get us down. I don't know if that's the same thing."

"Close enough," I said. "I'm not claustrophobic, but that feeling? Like everything's closing in on you . . . that's me. That's me, every day. For years. That's why I ended up in the hospital. I'd have these moments of being okay, but then I'd have these epic breakdowns. Like the other day at work. Go totally mental, or totally paralyzed. I mean, you've sort of seen it. So Mom and Dad put me in there."

"So what happened, how'd you get out?"

"The money ran out. Something like that. I don't know

how it all worked exactly, my dad was in charge. But some-times I want to go back. So I don't have to think, don't have to do anything. Just watch game shows and take meds and forget that Tara was ever my friend . . ."

I had to stop. My throat was tightening up.

"Pelly?"

I didn't respond. Just stared at the highway.

"You can say no," David said. "But—can I hug you?"

I still didn't respond. Then I dipped my chin down, once. Twice. So small, so slight, almost imperceptible.

Then his arms were around me, his ear pressed to mine. He just stood there, holding me. My hands rose all on their own and gripped his shoulders, squeezing. They were narrow but strong.

We stayed that way for a while. Eventually, though, when David didn't say anything else either, I got self-conscious. I let go of him, hopped off the hood, and started walking to the gas station's tiny convenience store. "You, um, want anything?"

"Mountain Dew," David said, like nothing had happened. "Thanks."

I waved a "no problem" back at him and went into the little shop.

Maybe David was right. Maybe I was shut off. Actually, no maybe about it. I kept people away, and yeah, I did it on pur-pose. What did that make me? Was I inhuman?

And what just happened out there? Between us. Did this mean—

"Shut up!" I shouted at the soda cooler.

Two customers turned and stared at me in shock. The cashier peered over a rack of chips to see what I was up to.

"I don't take back-sass from soda pop," I said to them.

Well, that didn't get a laugh, but it got them to turn away again. I grabbed a Dr Pepper and a Mountain Dew, paid hurriedly, and rushed back out to the car, where David was already behind the wheel.

"You all right?" David asked as he turned the engine.

I sputtered, trying to come up with an answer. And then I laughed. Hard. Bigger and bolder than anything so far today, than anything the past several years.

Back-sass from soda pop? Seriously?

I tried to explain myself and couldn't, curling up in the seat and holding my ribs. David started in with me, and for a while there, everything in the world was good.

TWELVE

"It, um . . . doesn't look terribly terrifying," David said, and then snorted like he'd surprised and amused himself with the wordplay.

"No," I said. "It doesn't."

We were parked across the street from Franklin Rebane's house in Canyon City.

Any other time, I might have admired the neighborhood. Tall pine trees lined every street, and the houses fell neatly into the "quaint" category. Mountains flanked Canyon City on three sides, and here in what Phoenicians called "the high country," the scrubby desert brush of Phoenix had disappeared, replaced by ancient trees of the Coconino National Forest. The streets waved up and down all through town, like pavement roller-coaster tracks, and Rebane's street was no different. His driveway tilted at a slight angle as it snaked around to the rear of the house.

We'd had no trouble finding it. Interstate 17 ran right
through the middle of town, with major streets branching off.
One of those branches led up a hill and into this neighborhood.
We'd stopped at a two-way intersection, driven straight up this
road called Rosemont, and there in the middle of the street sat
the house of the man who'd kidnapped my best friend.

The house itself was simple and, for lack of a better term,
"cute." Just like the others along Rosemont and the surrounding neighborhood. They were older clapboard models, many
whose chimneys had begun to tilt. A concrete path led from
the sidewalk to a raised porch and a red-painted front door.
The house was two stories but long and narrow, with an ancient
wood-shake shingled roof. I didn't see the white car anywhere,
but from where we were parked, also couldn't see to the back of
the house. It did seem like there was another building in back. A
workshop or small garage, maybe. We'd seen others like that at
other houses as we'd driven through the neighborhood.

"So now what?" David asked, and his voice had dropped as
if Rebane could somehow hear us.

"I don't honestly know."

"We could always just go up and ring the bell," David said.

"You're kidding, right?"

"Mmm . . . about seventy percent, yes. I mean, what are our
options here?"

"Wait till dark," I said. "Sneak in."

It didn't take long to feel the heat from David's eyes burning into the back of my head. I turned to face him.

"*Well,*" I said.

"Well, *what,*" David said. He wasn't smiling.

"Even if we got inside through the front door somehow, he'd recognize me from the Hole," I said. "And if he's Tara's kidnapper, he's not exactly going to give me a grand tour to prove it."

"He doesn't know me. I could go."

"He still isn't going to show you where he keeps her locked up."

David sank back into his seat and folded his arms so his hands were under his armpits. We'd both forgotten it's always about twenty degrees colder up here. David at least had an old 49ers football hoodie crumpled up behind his seat, but I didn't ask for it. I didn't even know he watched football.

"Yeah, speaking of where he keeps her locked up," David said, squinting out the window.

"What."

"Have you stopped to consider why, if that really was Tara—"

"It was!"

"—then why did he take her out in public like that?"

I raised my shoulders up to my ears, wrapping my arms tight around my stomach. "I don't know," I said. "Maybe he just figured no one would recognize her after so many years. Or he really wanted something to drink and didn't want to leave her alone in the car, I don't know."

"But why let her out *at all*, is what I'm saying."

"It doesn't matter!" I said. "He's a sicko psychopath whose balls should be cut off, that's it, that's the end of it, and he's got her in there somewhere, and I'm getting her out!"

I didn't realize how bitter and hateful I'd sounded saying all that until I glanced at David, whose eyes were wide as he stared at me.

That's when I noticed how hard my heart was pounding. I looked back at Rebane's house. Tried to calm my breathing. I used David's technique, counting four seconds to breathe in and six seconds to breathe out. Surprisingly, it actually seemed to help. I suddenly missed my meds again, though.

"Let's check out the rest of the neighborhood," I said, unable to look at Rebane's house anymore.

David released the brake, and we kept driving up Rosemont. The neighborhood was laid out in a simple loop. Rebane's street curved left and became a road called York. We followed York until I told David to stop. We were now west of Rebane's house—behind it.

"That's his roof," I said, pointing. "So the backyard of this house here must butt up against his. Look at that alley. We could walk right through there and end up at his backyard wall. Maybe there's something more we could see from the rear."

"Right now?"

"No. Tonight."

"You're serious."

"Well what the hell do you want me to do, David?"

David raised both hands. "Whoa," he said. "Easy there, boss. I'm on your side."

I covered my eyes. "Sorry," I said. "I didn't mean—"

"It's okay," David said, and put a hand on my leg. It almost surprised me that I didn't mind it. "Look, let's go get something to eat, huh? We can talk about it over burgers."

I had done nothing in my life to deserve being treated so well after barking like I did.

"Sure, burgers," I said. "Can we drive by his house just one more time?"

David nodded and drove us down York until we reached the two-way intersection where we'd first entered the neighborhood. He turned left to head back up Rosemont. As we went past Rebane's house again, I kept an eye out—looking for I'm not sure what. But other than a flurry of clouds starting to roll over the town, nothing had changed. I wondered if a storm was coming.

David and I didn't talk as he drove into what served as Canyon City's downtown. Really it was just a main drag down the 17, which through town was called—of course—Main Street. I pretended we were just focused on looking for a good place to eat, but it wasn't that kind of silence.

"There's an In-N-Out," David said, gesturing. "They're pretty good. How about we—"

"What's that?" I shouted, sitting up straight in my seat so fast the seat belt grabbed me back.

"What's what?" David said, slowing.

"Turn here," I said. "Turn right! Now!"

He did it, pulling into a parking lot and hitting the brakes. At the edge of the lot, beside the street, sat a monument-style sign. I glared at the white marquee with blue lettering and a simple geometric logo.

"That's it," I said. "That's the bumper sticker I saw on Rebane's car. The four Cs that looked like an Olympics logo."

I almost started laughing because it was so perfect and ridiculous and perfectly ridiculous.

The sign read CANYON CITY COMMUNITY CHURCH.

I scanned the parking lot, but it was mostly empty. I guess that made sense for a Saturday afternoon. None of the few cars parked there were Rebane's.

"Let's go in," I said.

"Okay, so, not opposed to this idea *per se*," David said. "But what's the plan?"

That stopped me. I didn't have what could rightly be called a "plan." Not until, as I was glancing around looking for inspiration, I saw a guy across the street coming out of a Mickey D's, wheeling a little girl in a stroller.

"Just follow my lead," I said, and got out of the car.

"You know, people say that on TV all the time, but does it really work?" David asked, shutting off the car and also climbing out.

"I don't know," I said. "I just always wanted to say it. Kind of feels badass."

David grinned and came around the truck to stand in front

of me. Before I knew what was happening, he'd tugged my chin toward his face and kissed me, once but nicely, on the lips.

It wasn't my first or anything. And it didn't make me get dizzy or weak in the knees or any of that melodramatic stuff.

But I felt it.

"Whoa," he said. "Um . . . I didn't mean to—"

"You should—" I interrupted, then had to stop and swallow. "Say something before doing that."

"I'm sorry," David said. "You're right. I just, I couldn't . . . yeah. I'm sorry."

"I mean, I would've said yes," I added. Which, honestly, surprised me. But when I said it, I knew it was true. I really don't know if I ever would have tried to kiss David Harowitz. Three days ago there'd be no way. The thought never would have occurred to me. Now, though . . . things were different.

"Yeah?" David asked. "You would've said yes?"

"I think so. But maybe not here. Or, *now*. I mean, we're in a church. For starters."

"We're in a parking lot," David said. "The church is over there. Can I kiss you? You said I should say something."

". . . Yeah, okay."

And he kissed me one more time. I'd been nervous to walk into the church building, but suddenly those nerves settled a bit. Or were at least replaced by a different type of nerves.

"Cool," David breathed. A little puff of frost sailed from his mouth.

"Cool," I said. "Okay."

It gave me the extra boost I needed to go inside the house of the Lord and lie to someone's face.

We followed signs to the main office and went in. An older lady at a desk looked up, assessed us with practiced ease, and chose to smile.

"Hello," she said pleasantly. "How can I help you?"

I'd never really done this before, but having come this far, *so* far, I forced myself to stay in character.

"Hi, I'm trying to locate Mr. Rebane?" I fought the urge to say more, figuring the more I talked, the more implausible my story would become. And I hated the way his name tasted in my mouth. It soured the vague peppermint David had breathed into me.

"Ooo, I don't believe Frank is on campus right now," the lady said. "He generally doesn't work on Saturday."

"Work?" I blurted before I could stop myself.

The lady looked confused at my confusion. Dammit.

"Well . . . yes," she said cautiously. "May I ask what this is about? I'd be happy to leave him a message."

This is right where I thought things might go. Time for the big reveal, see what happened.

"I'm friends with his daughter, from when we were little?" I said. "I've lost touch with her over the years, but I found out her dad went here, so I just thought I'd take a shot in the dark."

I tried to smile, and probably shouldn't have. I could feel the lie on my face.

But I got the answer I needed.

The lady slowly shook her head. "I'm sorry," she said. "Frank has no children. He's never been married."

Yes! I thought. *I've got you, you son of a bitch.*

"Oh," I said, hoping my surprise was at least a little convincing. "I guess . . . you're sure? I mean, of course you'd be sure, it's just that I . . . I must've gotten the wrong Mr. Rebane entirely. Wow. I'm so sorry."

My acting skills weren't so bad after all—the lady smiled kindly and said it was no problem. David and I thanked her and walked quickly back to the car. As if on instinct, neither of us said anything until we were both inside and the doors closed.

"No children," I said. "So he lied. That wasn't his daughter. I knew it!"

"You're talking about at the Hole," David clarified.

"Yes. He said, 'I'll have a short decaf, and my daughter will have a hot chocolate.'"

David nodded thoughtfully, but even as he did, I felt my resolve slipping. It must've shown on my face, because David then said, "What?"

"I don't know," I said. "I, um . . . that's maybe not the exact wording he used."

David arched an eyebrow. I rubbed my face. God, this was getting complicated.

"He might've just said, 'and *she'll* have.' Maybe he never actually said she was his daughter. I mean, if he'd said *that* and he doesn't have kids, then he lied. Maybe I could take that to the cops and it would raise a little more hell."

"But if he didn't say 'daughter'—"

"If he didn't say 'daughter,' then he's just an old guy with some girl. Could be her uncle, a family friend. Maybe he's her youth pastor."

"Yeah, what was that whole him-working-here thing," David said. "You looked surprised when she said that."

"I was. I am. I had no idea. I don't know what he does here. You think he works with kids?" The thought churned my stomach.

"Who knows," David said. "What's our next move?"

I didn't miss the fact that he said "our" instead of "your," and it was kind of awesome. Just as a side note.

"I still think we need to stake out his house or something," I said. "That's where the answers are."

"Well, I don't recommend we do that till it's dark," David said. "And we've got a couple hours before that happens. Let's stick with grabbing food for the moment, huh? We can talk about our options."

"Okay, yeah," I said.

David started up the truck and drove us back toward the In-N-Out. As he was parking, I said, "Did we . . . just . . . kiss? Back there?"

"Um, yes," David said. He shut off the engine. "Is that still okay? We actually did it twice, I don't know if you were counting."

"No, I remember," I said. "I'm just trying to figure out what that means."

"Well," David said. "When you figure it out, let me know. Because, um, I'm pretty much, like, *high* right now. I kind of can't feel my legs."

I wrinkled my nose. "Really?"

He laughed. "Really, yeah. It's kind of trippy."

"Is it totally weird we're having this conversation while planning to stake out a kidnapper's house?"

"Totally," David agreed. "Hamburgers?"

Being up here in Canyon City, trying to find my best friend, possibly confronting what I felt was pure evil . . . I was scared. I was worried. I was nervous. I was afraid nothing would come out of it.

And at that moment, I knew I liked David Harowitz as more than a friend after all.

"Sure," I said. "Hamburgers."

THIRTEEN

We drove back to Rebane's neighborhood half an hour after sunset. We'd eaten dinner, which wasn't easy for me, as my guts kept going topsy-turvy inside every time I thought too much about where we were and what we were doing.

Looking for Tara, I mean. Not having dinner with David. That part was pretty cool despite the circumstances.

David insisted we stop for more warm clothes, and I didn't argue. A Walmart provided us with cheap knit gloves, scarves, and caps. I was glad to pull something warm over my head, and the plain black scarf warmed my breath when I wrapped it across my mouth. I wouldn't have thought to get that stuff. Thank God for David.

Finally we drove past Rebane's house again. We saw lights on now, glowing through a set of gauzy curtains in a picture window, but I still didn't see his car.

"I want to go around the other side," I told David. "To that alley we saw earlier. See if we can look into the backyard."

"We should park down the road a bit, then," David said. "Walk to the alley."

"How come?"

"So it doesn't look like we're, you know. Parking by an alley to go walking through it to someone's backyard wall."

"Yeah, okay."

We chose a dirt area off the residential street at the bottom of the hill. Together David and I began trudging up York Street, the road west of Rebane's.

"Is it getting colder?" I asked, shivering as we walked.

"Yeah," David said, and a plume of his breath billowed out in a fine white cloud. Then he stopped and looked up. "And, um, snowing."

I stopped beside him and lifted my hands out of the 49ers hoodie. In the darkness I hadn't noticed it, but once David pointed it out, I could feel little ice kisses raining down here and there on my face. It almost tickled.

"Wow," I said quietly, momentarily setting aside my mission.

"Yeah," David echoed. "Can I hold your hand?"

"What?"

"Your hand," David said. "May I hold it."

"Oh," I said, and, absurdly, held up my right hand as if to make sure it was still there. There were no streetlights except for one right at the entrance to the street. "Um. Yeah. Sure."

David wrapped his long fingers around my palm. My hand was practically buried in his. And for some reason that simple contact, even through the knit cotton gloves, made me want to cry.

"Hey," David said gently. "You okay?"

"Y-yes," I said. My voice shook, drawing the single syllable out to several.

"We can stop," David said. He held up our joined hands.

"No," I said, running the sleeve of my left arm under my nose. "I'd really rather not."

We hiked together up the hill and took a left. While the light from the quaint houses looked warm and inviting, I don't think any of them could possibly have been as warm as I felt right then with David.

My warmth cooled when we reached the alley. I didn't feel panicky, but it was in the mail. David and I both glanced around. All the houses seemed sealed up against the chill. Without a word, we nodded to each other and walked briskly down the dirt alley.

I realized quickly it was less an alley and more of a stretch of dead earth that maybe had served as a driveway long ago for a house that had since been torn down. Following it, we ended up at a brown cinderblock wall I recognized as the same style and color as that which surrounded Rebane's house on two sides. This was it.

David stood on tiptoe, but tall evergreen bushes ran the entire length of the wall on the yard side of Rebane's property, like natural camouflage. David dropped back down and shook his head.

"Can't see through the bushes," he whispered.

"Boost me up," I said.

David looked uncertain but then cupped his hands. I put my right foot in his hands and he shoved me upward. I was able to hold myself up with my arms while I peered through the greens.

It was Rebane's place, all right. The car was parked on a concrete slab facing out, like he'd backed into place. I'd been right about there being another building; a garage or workshop sat on my right in the corner, backed against the wall. I could make out a rectangle of light coming from a back door, but couldn't see well enough to tell what kind of room it led to. Concrete steps led down from the door, ending a few feet from the rear bumper of the car. There were no lights on upstairs. The same tall bushes lined the other two walls surrounding the house.

Between the detached garage and the house, by the light of the back window, I saw he had a remarkably nice garden filled with pretty little flowers. I have to admit, that part caught me off guard. How did he keep them alive in the cold? It wasn't the kind of thing I expected from a kidnapper.

Unless, of course, he isn't one, someone in my head told me.

I shook my head to clear it.

"Okay," I whispered.

David loosened his grip and then slid his hands along the

outside of my legs and waist as I dropped to the ground, making sure I didn't fall on my rear. Or maybe taking the opportunity to get a little friendly with his hands. Either way was fine with me. Why was this happening *now*?

"Well?" he said as we leaned against the wall and went back to scanning for anyone who might be sneaking up on us.

I frowned. "How tall are you?"

"About six foot."

"So then the wall is what?"

"Just a bit over that."

"And the bushes go up another couple feet," I said. "There's a detached garage in that corner, but his car isn't parked in it. It's parked by the back door. He could drive back there and get someone into or out of the house without anyone seeing."

"So he's a private guy," David said. And when I glared at him, he added, "Just playing devil's advocate. A little while ago you were joking about breaking and entering."

I hadn't been joking. And thought the better of mentioning it. Instead I said, "I thought you were on my side."

"I'm freezing my ass off in a dark alley in Canyon City to spy on an alleged kidnapper," David said. He kicked my shoe. "Pretty sure I'm on your side."

"Fair enough," I said.

Also, he was right: it was getting colder. Snow still drifted down and piled up ever so gently against phone poles and sidewalk curbs. Not big drifts or anything, and it would probably be gone by morning, but still.

"So what now, Sherlock?" David said, rubbing his hands together.

I almost told him we should get back to his car, blast the heater, and go get some superhot coffee, because I didn't have a single other idea in mind. The fact that we—that *I*—had even gotten this far seemed something just short of miraculous.

Yet all I had to show for our trouble today was that according to his church, Franklin Rebane didn't have a daughter. A fact that by itself meant absolutely nothing. Maybe gathering more intelligence was the way to go, do more research on him. Or maybe we were best served just going home and seeing what the police came up with.

Instead of saying any of this, I shut my mouth and pressed my lips together as I heard the back door to Rebane's house open and close.

David and I locked eyes.

I heard keys jingling, that same irritating pocket-jingle from the Hole in the Wall. A moment later I heard him get into the car, start it up, and then roll down the driveway.

He'd left.

I can only imagine what my face must've looked like, because David very quickly said, "Hold on, Pel."

"No, come on," I said. "I've got to go *now*."

"Pelly, wait."

"We won't get another shot like this. David, please!"

"Then I'm coming with you."

"I need you around the corner to watch for him, so you can

call me when he comes back," I said. "Just, come on! Boost me over, I want to look through the windows."

"And then what?"

"Then I'll run down to the street or find a way back over the wall. David, hurry!"

Shaking his head, David again boosted me up, only this time I swung one leg over the wall.

"Go," I said.

"You're sure?"

"Yes, go!"

David went quickly down the alley, swiveling his head at the surrounding houses, then took a right and headed up the street. I knew from our surveillance that he'd follow the curve until it became Rebane's street.

Perfect.

Getting down off the wall wasn't quite as tough as I'd suspected. I grabbed the top and let myself hang down, then dropped. I got a few scrapes along my arms but nothing major. I was now crouched in the bushes facing the back side of Rebane's house.

I crawled carefully out from the foliage. Skittered over to the garage. The double doors faced the house and garden, padlocked with a length of heavy chain through the door handles. I gave the lock a tug just in case, but no dice. Then, like an idiot, I let the lock clatter against the doors, and winced. I looked all around, waiting for a dog to bark or lights to pop on around me. That's when I realized the houses on either side of Rebane's were likewise blocked by his tall bushes. No way for anyone to see into the yard without poking up over the wall like David and I had done. I doubted many people peeked over walls in this neighborhood.

I hurried over to the back door and peered inside. Rebane had left the light on.

I wrapped my scarf around my mouth to warm my breath, which came out like a dog on a hot day. I was used to panic, or as used to it as a person can get. That's not what this was. This was . . .

Excitement.

Don't get me wrong, I was terrified. But I wasn't curled up in bed, or pacing and smoking and muttering, or in a stupid mental hospital. I was doing. I was *acting*.

And also clearly more insane than I'd ever really believed. I shouldn't even be here, I'm going to get caught or worse, and—

"No, hang in there," I whispered to myself. The scarf still tasted like the smell of Walmart. "You can do this. You can do this for her."

The door led to a little portion of the kitchen, basically just a short hallway. A washer and dryer sat against the left wall next to a countertop and drawers. The right-hand wall consisted of several rows of shelving and a large pantry door, probably a walk-in.

Heart beating madly, I risked trying the doorknob. Just to tell myself later I'd done it. Just to know I'd had the guts.

It turned readily and silently in my hand.

I sucked in a breath. Did he live with anyone else? What about a dog—did he have a huge mastiff waiting to pounce? Where had he gone, how long did I have?

Tara, I told myself. *Tara might be in here, you have to at least see, David will let you know if he's coming back.*

And come back he would. Probably soon, I figured, because nobody leaves their doors unlocked unless they're coming home quickly. Actually, I didn't know anyone who left their doors unlocked at all. But Canyon City wasn't exactly a pirate cove of nefarious activity.

Why would a kidnapper leave his door open? Maybe because he wasn't . . . ?

Everything in my mind and soul said to go in, to prove the truth, to find Tara. Everything in my body said to go *home.* Right the hell now, because I'd never been more wrong about anything in my life.

Except as I crouched there panting into my scarf, I realized that while my symptoms were the same as my trusty panic attacks, I wasn't panicking.

I was . . . in control.

Screw it. May as well ride this pony while I could. I opened the door and put my head inside, listening.

Nothing. Just the natural hum of electricity from a house that's lived in.

I crept inside and shut the door behind me. I couldn't feel my limbs anymore, and my heart gave only one thunderous pound per minute.

The window in the door, divided into nine equal panes, had a rolling shade, which was open. The drawstring tapped against the glass as I closed the door, scaring me nearly to death. I stepped slowly across faded yellow linoleum flooring toward the kitchen.

The house smelled vaguely of something sweet. Some kind of vanilla. Kind of nice, really. The kitchen seemed fairly normal. Not to use a broad brush, but it was pretty clear right off that no woman was in charge here. Dishes lay unwashed in the sink, and the glass-doored cabinets revealed staples like ramen noodles, canned spaghetti sauce, and dry cereal and oatmeal.

I stepped carefully into the living room. Redbrick fireplace, small flat-screen TV in front of a recliner, and a couch with paleolithic upholstery. Empty mug on a TV tray beside the recliner. I got the feeling if I touched the TV, it would still be warm.

I slid farther into the room with every nerve on red alert. Impulsively I grabbed the remote off the TV tray and pressed the power button. The flatscreen popped to life.

The Discovery Channel. *MythBusters*.

Something rippled across the back of my neck, like little spider legs. I turned, expecting Rebane to be standing there staring at me, but he wasn't. Instead I saw a series of small, framed photos on the wall. Family photos, it looked. I didn't see anyone who looked like a wife, but I saw several pictures of two boys. Nephews, maybe. Or sons from a marriage gone south . . .

My neck tickled again. One single word whispered through my brain.

Wrong.

I was so wrong.

Slowly I turned in a tight circle, scanning the whole room. White curtains closed over a large picture window beside the front door. A staircase led up to the second floor. I considered going up there to continue my investigation, but couldn't. Because I was wrong.

I don't know what I'd been looking for, but it wasn't here. Not a single thing here said "girl." Kidnapped or otherwise. Franklin Rebane was a bachelor. An old-school, semi-retired bachelor, and that was all.

I hadn't actually seen Franklin Rebane yet today. The driver of the car could've been a friend. A friend who had a daughter who looked like Tara. Or it *had* been Rebane at the café, but the girl just went to his church or something.

Whatever. Didn't matter. I'd made a horrible mistake. That's what mattered.

I'd just turned the television off when I heard a car pulling into the driveway out back.

The oxygen in my lungs froze like the snowflakes falling outside. The freeze twirled down my legs and paralyzed me.

Rebane was back.

I moved on some bizarre autopilot. Shuffled my ice-block feet backward in the living room. Into a corner, so that the entrance from the kitchen was on my left. Once against the wall, I didn't move another muscle except for those around my eyes. Sent them darting in every direction looking for another escape. I could dive through the picture window, but that probably only worked in the movies. The front door was farther away, but I could make it if I ran now, now, *now* . . .

The kitchen door opened. Closed.

Rebane cleared his throat. Hummed a foreign tune. Maybe a hymn.

Coming this way.

Of course he was coming this way. Where else was there to go?

Please don't see me, I prayed as if to Rebane.

Please just don't see me and I'll go right back out the way I came and we'll forget this ever happened okay just please don't see me oh my God please don't see me.

Rebane walked into the living room. Definitely the man from the café.

He jingled his keys. *Jang, jang, jang.*

Lots of people jingle their keys, I thought. *Hundreds. Thousands. That was your evidence? Your proof? You're going to go to prison over a noisy key ring?*

Rebane turned left. Away from my corner.

He bounded up the stairs, carrying a white plastic drugstore bag. Pretty good shape for an old guy. From where I stood trembling, the stairs turned Rebane's profile to me as he climbed. Surely he'd see the cowering girl in the corner of his living room, surely . . .

His head, chest, legs, feet—one step at a time he disappeared upstairs.

Thank you thank you thank you.

But I couldn't run.

I wanted to. Knew it might make too much noise. Also, I just *couldn't*. The adrenaline in my quads locked them in place, and it was a miracle I could even walk. My feet felt like they were being sucked down by playground sand. If he caught me, I would go to jail. Period. The end. I thought being on a school campus would be hard? Imagine me in prison . . .

I shuffled into the kitchen, unable to pick my feet up off the floor. I considered hiding in the pantry. Discarded it. The pantry door had a padlock on it, slipped through a hinged bracket lock. Probably kept his booze there.

My eyes offered only tunnel vision of the back kitchen door. They seemed to zoom in and focus on the window-shade drawstring. It swung faintly back and forth from Rebane's entrance moments ago.

The door is unlocked, I told myself. *Just open it and slip out and you're safe—*

Upstairs, Rebane cleared his throat again. I heard his full ring of keys land on a table. The sound triggered my muscles. I moved.

I quick-stepped back into the short hallway. Past the washer and dryer. Reached the kitchen door. Grabbed the doorknob. Twisted.

The knob didn't move.

Footsteps on the staircase.

Oh God. Oh God. Please. Stop. No.

Pushed my fingers dumbly against the doorknob lock. Gloves still on. Slipping off the lock. Couldn't get a grip.

The living room floor creaked behind me. A moment later I heard Adam and Jamie on *MythBusters* talking about blowing something up.

I peeled off my glove. Managed to get a grip on the lock. Tried the knob again. It turned easily.

I pulled the door open halfway. Pivoted through the doorway. Shut it behind me as carefully as I could.

Then I sprinted for the back wall, crashed through the bushes where I'd come out, and somehow managed to jam one foot in between a couple of thick branches and launch myself at the wall, the impact jarring my held breath out of me in a hack. I hadn't breathed for several minutes.

I jumped down into the alley and took off at a run for the street, praying I wouldn't throw up or wet my pants or die or all three, in any order. I followed the curve to Rosemont in no time at all, coming onto Rebane's street just as David was about to knock on the front door.

"David!" I wheezed.

Somehow he heard me in the drifting snowfall and rushed toward me. I collapsed into his arms.

"You okay?" he said quickly.

I groaned into his chest, "Go."

Without a word, David picked me up in his arms like a

baby doll and practically skied down the street to the truck. He put me in the passenger seat, then ran around and climbed in beside me.

"What happened?" he said. His eyes were wide and wild.

Panic crawled up and down my spine with hypodermic legs, piercing each vertebrae. Comparing it to a heart attack wouldn't do it justice. There were the day-to-day attacks I'd had for the last six years, ever since Tara was taken. This was not that. This was worse. So much for my big recovery.

My entire body shook as I curled up on the passenger seat. My eyelids froze open, staring senselessly at the dashboard but not seeing it. My jaw wrenched shut, my breath wheezing from between the spaces in my teeth. I may have been muttering, I may have been screaming—no way to know.

"Pelly?"

David's voice came from a mile away. When he touched my arm, I screeched and shrank farther into myself, covering my head with both arms. After that I was paralyzed. Couldn't move if my life depended on it.

"Okay," David said. "Okay, we're going home. Pelly? I'm gonna get us home, okay?"

I hated him. I hated David like fire consuming the snow.

"You were supposed to tell me he was coming," I hissed at him, my teeth still tightly clenched together.

"I did!" David said. "I called twice."

My muscles relaxed enough for me to pull out my phone to show him how wrong he was.

It wouldn't turn on. I tried again and again, and even took the battery out and put it back. Nothing.

If he'd caught you, I thought, *he'd have called the cops, and kept you there till they showed up, and you wouldn't even have been able to call anyone. You stupid idiot.* My rubber band wouldn't be enough to change my intrusive thoughts this time. It wasn't punishment enough. Maybe a good flogging would come closer. Maybe a tumble down a mountain.

David looked at my dead phone. He sighed, shut his eyes, and leaned against the seat. "Jesus, that was close. He could've caught you snooping around his yard."

"He almost did," I whispered. "He came in while I was in the living room—"

"Living room?" David squeaked. "You went *inside* the house?!"

"The kitchen door was unlocked."

David stared hard at me. For a second I was reminded of my dad when he was pissed.

"Are you crazy?" David said.

"Yes. I tried to tell you that."

David plowed ahead. I don't think he'd heard me.

"You are absolutely *freaking* insane!" David said. "Dammit, Pelly! You want to get your ass thrown in jail, that's fine, but I'm not coming with you. I cannot believe you broke into his house. Did you find Tara? Huh? Did you?"

That strange hate I'd just felt toward him disappeared. Replaced by guilt.

"No," I said. "No, she's not there, it's not him—"

"Oh, it's not?" David snapped. "The old man in that house isn't a kidnapper? Really? Gee, ya think?"

"I'm sorry," I whispered.

He looked like he wanted to say more. Instead he sat back in his seat and looked out his window. His right hand grabbed the steering wheel. Gripped it hard, relaxed. Gripped it again. Relaxed.

After a minute David said, "How did you not notice your cell was dead?"

"I'm sorry," I said again, staring blankly at the dashboard. "I'm so dumb, I'm sorry, I didn't think, I just wanted her back to make it all stop and instead it didn't and look at me, David, look at how stupid I am—"

"Hey, hey," David said, turning. When he touched my arm again, I didn't flinch. "Stop. It's all right, Pel. You're safe. I shouldn't have yelled at you."

"Yes, you should," I said. "Everyone should."

"Pelly, don't."

"It's my fault."

"What's your fault?"

"It's my fault Tara's gone. He should've taken me. It should've been me—"

"What are you talking about?"

I wanted my meds back. I wanted a pill, something to take to put me out, put me down. I'd hidden this part of the story so far away, for so very long, it had spoiled and turned rotten. It had burned a hole in me somewhere that nothing could ever fix.

I pulled out my cigarettes and lighter, my fingers grazing my pillbox during the procedure. I really felt like bleeding but couldn't do that now. Smoking would have to do. I lit the Camel and rolled down my window about halfway. Pretty little snowflakes darted inside. David said nothing.

"He talked to me first," I said.

David folded his arms, putting his hands under his armpits.

"I was watching Tara from behind a rack of skirts," I said. "And someone came up behind me and said, 'Excuse me, do you like dogs?' I didn't even turn around. I just waved my hand and said no. And he said . . . he said he just bought a cute little puppy from the mall pet store, but he'd jumped out of the car and was loose somewhere in the parking garage, and he needed help to find him. Well, I could see Tara looking for me. You know, all cautious? And I laughed. And I told the guy I couldn't, because I was busy, I was hiding. Then Tara ran for another rack of clothes and I lost sight of her. The guy said, okay, well, thank you anyway, I hope you don't get caught."

"So, you think that's the guy who took her."

"I'm positive."

"And you never got a look at him?"

I practically spat out a breath of smoke. "I was irritated," I said. "I was focused on the game. I wasn't thinking about stranger danger or anything like that. I was ten. I was a big girl. No. I never got a look. But it was him."

"How do you know?"

"Haven't you ever heard of that trick? The lost dog? Bad guys use it all the time. I guess it still works. Trust me, it was him. What I don't know is . . . I don't know why . . . Jesus, why wasn't it me?"

I took another drag. David shifted in his seat to get a better look at my face. So I turned away. Let the snow freeze my cheeks.

"That's what this was all about," David said. It wasn't a question. "You think it should've been you he took. Or you think you could've stopped him somehow."

"If we hadn't been playing that stupid game, or if I'd just turned around and looked at this guy, or—"

"No, no, Pelly," David said. "God, no. You can't do this. You can't live like that. Tara is gone because some creeper asshole took her. And you want to know why? Because that's what creeper assholes *do*. That is not your fault. Then, now, or ever."

"It sure feels like it."

"Pel, listen," David said. "I'm going to say this because—well, I guess it doesn't matter why, but I have to say it. You understand that it's almost certain you imagined this whole thing, now, right? I mean, seeing Tara at the Hole?"

I inhaled smoke. Held it. Blew it out.

"I mean, the *chances*," David went on. "Just the math of it. It's virtually impossible. I mean, you get that, right?"

Inhale. Hold. Exhale. At least I had no intrusive thoughts. I had no thoughts at all.

After another minute, since I wasn't responding to David, he pressed his lips together and started the truck. "We're out of here," he said. "We're going home."

I didn't say anything. Just flicked my smoke out the window and rolled the window back up. I sat, and shook and hoped to someday be able to speak again.

David drove a little fast out of the neighborhood, and once, the truck skidded a bit on the wet street. I didn't care, and David didn't appear to either. But that minor fishtail did pull me back to the present, to the now, and right now I needed him to slow down.

"Easy," I muttered.

"What?"

"Go easy," I said. "Slow down some."

Immediately the truck slowed. "Sorry."

I shook my head. "S'okay."

We said nothing more for at least a couple of minutes. Outside, snow fell and with it, silence, a cloud of it, draping the entire landscape. It never snowed at home.

"So, since you did go in," David said at last, "what'd you find? Anything?"

"No," I said. I pulled myself up, slowly, into a sitting position and pulled on my seat belt. My voice sounded monotone and splintered. "The garage was locked. The kitchen was normal. Living room was normal. He's the blandest person on earth."

"Hmm," David grunted, but that was all.

I rubbed my eyes. "I don't have anything else."

And for the first time in a while, so long they were like foreign objects piercing my corneas, tears formed in my eyes and burned like acid.

David must've seen them even though they didn't fall. He put a hand on my shoulder. "Hey, Pel," he said. "You did more than any person would be expected to. You followed your gut—your *heart*—and you risked a lot to find out. Maybe too much, honestly. You shouldn't have gone in there. I mean, I get it, I would've done it too. I'm just saying, you went above and beyond, Pelly. The cops'll still look into it, like you said. There's nothing else for us to do."

I didn't miss that he said "us." And that almost made the sudden tears fall after all.

"I don't check my phone," I said, as if unable to stop myself, "because no one calls. I don't have any friends. Just people online whose names I don't know, and that girl who buys my fucking cigarettes . . . I don't want to even hear the voice mails my dad leaves. That's why I didn't notice it was dead."

That's why my phone never seemed to have a charge. For as terrified as I was of not having it work, the truth was, knowing it wouldn't ever ring felt worse.

"Okay," David said softly.

"I was on medication for the last five years. I stopped taking it."

David looked unperturbed. I guess after telling him about the hospital, meds weren't exactly a shock. Maybe that's why I was telling him. I had nothing left to hide.

"When?" he asked.

"A few weeks ago."

"Okay."

"I don't want to be shut off."

We came to a red light. David leaned over and kissed my forehead, then my lips.

"Okay," he said firmly.

Somehow that made everything . . . well, okay.

The light turned green, and David hit the gas. We passed the church where Rebane worked, hit a yellow light, and then things quickly became decidedly not okay as David tried to stop for the red.

The truck spun out, fishtailing this way and that. I screamed. David grunted and fought for control.

He lost.

FOURTEEN

We bounced off the freeway, through snow-covered dirt and gravel, and smashed headlong into a telephone pole.

"Oh my God," I said, and proceeded to repeat this about eight trillion times in the span of a minute or two. I did not want to look at the driver's seat, where I was sure I would find David either ejected out the windshield or simply a bloody remnant impaled on the steering wheel.

I knew neither was true. It didn't prevent the specter from haunting me.

"Are you all right?" David asked right away. He sounded fine.

"Yeah, I—yeah. Are you?"

"Yeah. Pretty sure . . . yeah."

"Pretty sure isn't gonna do it for me these days, David."

"I'm fine," he stated. He peered through the windshield,

which wasn't so much as cracked. "So, ah . . . not used to driving in the snow, I guess."

"I guess," I agreed as I began to accept that we were both alive and whole. "You're sure—"

"Totally. Sit tight, I'll take a look."

He unsnapped his belt and got out of the car. The peel out had taken us completely off the road, which was good; we were probably twenty or more feet from passing cars, although traffic was light, probably due to the snow. David lifted the hood up and tinkered for a minute before walking quickly to his door, hands shoved deep in his jeans pockets and arms held tight to his body. I would've laughed at the way his face pinched in the falling snow if I was in a psychological place where I could laugh at anything.

David climbed inside and tried the ignition. Nothing.

"That's kinda what I thought," he said. "We're gonna need a tow."

"Awesome," I said. "I hope *your* phone is charged."

David smirked at me just as the truck got lit up by headlights pulling up behind us. My heart twisted for a second, thinking we were about to be hit. But I watched in the mirror, then turned in my seat, as a man driving a full-size pickup truck stopped behind David's and got out to approach David's window. He knocked on it, and David rolled it down.

"You okay in there?" the man asked. He was older, his skin weather-worn.

"We're fine, thank you," David said. "The truck's busted up pretty good, though."

The old man nodded. "Need a tow, then, do ya?"

"I was about to call, yeah."

"We'll wait here till ya get it sorted out. Hit your hazards if they're working."

"Right, thanks," David said, and turned on his blinkers. The old man walked back to the big pickup and climbed in. "Nice guy," David said, taking out his phone.

"Uh-huh," I said. I leaned back in the seat and shut my eyes. Now that the worst of the panic had passed, I was both hungry and nauseated. Saltines sounded awesome.

David called the police and then AAA. When he was done, he held the phone toward me. "Need to call your mom?"

Yikes. I probably did. I should at least let her know where I was.

It took a few minutes for me to remember the number, during which the cops arrived, asked a few questions and took a report, laughed a bit at our inability to drive a car in the snow, and left once the tow truck showed up.

Mom didn't answer the phone. It made sense; she wouldn't have David's number on her cell, and probably figured if it was someone important, they'd leave a voice mail.

"Mom, it's me," I said. "I'm, uh . . ."

So. How to explain this little situation?

I decided I couldn't. Not now, anyway. I was safe, she knew I was with David, and she'd lose her mind if I told her exactly what I'd been up to today. They'd probably take out a second mortgage to pay for me to go right back into the hospital.

"I'm working late at the café," I went on. "There's this huge art group or something coming through, and Eli needs me to stay all night, so I won't be home till late. Don't stay up. Um, my cell is out, so you can reach me at this number, it's my . . . friend . . . David. You know, from work. Okay. Bye."

I ended the call and went out to stand beside David and the tow-truck driver.

The driver agreed right away with David's assessment of *I can't start my freaking car*. Genius.

"We're gonna hafta take it in," the driver said. "You wanna take it to my shop, or somewhere else?"

"How long will it take to fix?" David asked, teeth chattering a bit.

The driver shook his head. "Tomorrow. *Late* tomorrow. If even then. You really whacked her."

"Wow," David said.

"I could call my mom back, get us a ride back to Phoenix," I said, shivering.

David put an arm around me. "Will you get in trouble?"

"I haven't been in trouble in six years," I said as my body warmed up just a bit beneath his arm.

"Whatcha wanna do?" the driver asked impatiently.

"Sorry, yes, take it in," David said. "Thanks."

The driver gave him a business card and began hooking the red truck up to the tow.

"I can call a friend or two," David said as we watched the Toyota getting jacked up. "Or we could try to find a place here, go back home tomorrow."

"Here?" I repeated. "Like, a hotel?"

In different rooms? I wondered. Wouldn't that be expensive? Or the same room? And if the same room, then would we share the same—

The burly, older man climbed out of the big truck behind ours and came over while I was still stuttering internally.

"Why don't you two hop on in here," the good Samaritan said, gesturing back to the pickup. "You're going to be Popsicles."

David and I looked at each other. I tried to signal "no" with my eyes; I didn't exactly cherish the idea of getting into a stranger's car after everything that had happened. But whether David didn't catch my look, or just chose to countermand it, he said, "Sure, thanks," and the next thing I knew, we were climbing into the rear of the man's double cab.

A knit blanket lay folded on the bench seat. David opened the blanket and passed it over to me. I gratefully laid it across my lap. If we were going to get ax-murdered by this old guy, I at least wanted to be warm.

Then I couldn't help but gasp when a little elderly woman in the passenger seat turned to face us.

"The Lord sure works in mysterious ways, hmm?" she said. It was the secretary from Canyon City Community Church.

"Fancy seeing you out here," she went on. "I'm Mrs. Wallis, and this is Kirk."

"Hey-o," Kirk Wallis said with a nod as he shut his door.

David and I were both speechless for a second, contemplating this bizarre twist of fate. He recovered first, and introduced us.

"I can't tell you how much we appreciate this," David added as the ice in my body began to melt.

"Me too," I added, feeling inadequate. But I also felt my skin stop crawling; these were two ordinary old folks, one of whom worked at a church. They couldn't possibly be dangerous.

Just like Franklin Rebane, my inner voice sassed me. I snapped my rubber band to shut it up.

"We're just sorry about your car," Mrs. Wallis said.

"It'll be ready late tomorrow," David said. "Can you recommend a cheap place we could stay for the night, by chance?"

"Why, you'll stay with us, of course," Mrs. Wallis said.

"Oh no," I said, too quickly to be polite, and I didn't care. "We couldn't—"

"Sweetheart," Mrs. Wallis said, "I've been a mother, a third-grade teacher, and a police dispatcher, and I teach junior high Sunday School. Which is to say, you can't change my mind once it's made up."

I shot David a look. He shrugged and tried hard not to smile too big. "Can't argue with that," he said.

"Exactly," Mrs. Wallis said. "I'm just too darn stubborn."

"And humble," her husband said, and laughed.

She joined him, and so did David, and for the briefest of moments . . . I hated them. Envy and bitterness and misplaced resentment combined in my guts to make a fermented bile that almost sickened me. I'd never have this again, this family thing, this laughing at dumb jokes and doing things together.

But then I suppose neither would Tara.

Tara. I tried, I really did. I thought for sure . . .

In my bitterness I said, "Oh, no, thank you so much, but it's fine, really, we'll get a motel or something."

"Oh?" Mrs. Wallis said, raising her eyebrows innocently. "So you're married, are you?"

Great. I guess there were one or two drawbacks to Christian hospitality.

"Not exactly," I said. "I mean, no, we're not, I mean, this was just supposed to be a day trip, you know, it wasn't like we were planning on . . . anything. You know."

"Well then, we insist," Mrs. Wallis said. "It's far too late and too cold for you to be running around out there anyway, and I won't let Kirk drive you anywhere but our home. You're both more than welcome."

I glanced again at David. He seemed totally and utterly amused by the entire situation.

"Sounds great," David said. "Thank you so much."

"Thanks," I mumbled.

It took another fifteen minutes or so for the tow-truck driver to finish getting the little red truck hooked up and taken away. Under any other circumstance, I wouldn't be caught in a stranger's car going to God knows where in a city that wasn't even mine. But I had David, and I was exhausted by the night's events. *And* we held hands under the blanket the entire way. He seemed at ease, which worked wonders on my own state of mind.

Right up until we made a turn onto a street I was already familiar with.

David didn't miss it either. We both sat up a bit. The road we'd turned onto lay only a few blocks from Rebane's neighborhood. Just as I thought for sure it would end up they were neighbors, and maybe even had plans to turn me and David over to him, Mr. Wallis made another turn and, just like that, we were moving away from Rebane's house.

I sighed inwardly, grateful as we pulled up to the driveway of the Wallises' house. It was the same basic design as Rebane's, which is to say the same as most of the houses in the area, as far as I could tell. Mr. Wallis parked beside the house, not in the back, which was nice; much less spooky for me. On a pleasant day I guessed it would be maybe a twenty-minute walk, at most, from here to Rebane's house.

"Here we are," Mr. Wallis announced.

We bundled out of the truck and followed them to the front door. A warm burst of air greeted us first thing, followed by an aromatic hint of balsam and cedar.

"I'll get started on some hot chocolate," Mrs. Wallis said as she hung her coat on a rack beside the door.

"And I'll see who won the game," Mr. Wallis said, and thumped David on the back.

"We have a spare room upstairs for you, Penelope," Mrs.

Wallis said, bustling through the living room and into the kitchen. The layout was identical to Rebane's house and made me jumpy. I felt like I was breaking and entering all over again.

"Right," I said. "Sure, yes. Thank you."

"And I'll make up the futon in the basement for David," she went on, calling now from the kitchen. "It's right this way."

"Sounds great," David said, walking toward the kitchen doorway while Mr. Wallis tried to find his sports game.

But I stopped dead as I saw Mrs. Wallis unlatch a half-door, kind of a gate, at the top of a set of stairs beside the kitchen door.

"Basement?" I said.

"Oh, it's not so bad," Mrs. Wallis said, waving at me. "It's finished. There's heat and a bathroom. No shower, but there's always the guest bath. I'm sure this young man will be just fine. I'll even put on an extra comforter."

"Perfect," David said.

I took one step closer to the kitchen but didn't cross the threshold. I couldn't have even if I wanted to. My legs quivered fearfully as I asked her, "Do, um . . . do all the houses around here have basements?"

"Well, I don't know for certain," Mrs. Wallis said. "But in this area all the houses were built by . . . oh, shoot, Kirk? What was the name of the family who built all the—"

"Daniels," Kirk said from the living room. "Maurice Daniels and Sons. Did about half this side of the mountain years back."

"Daniels, that's right," Mrs. Wallis said. "They developed a large portion of this side of Canyon City." She looked over at me. "Several of our neighbors have the same floor plan as ours," she added, and shrugged. "They have basements as well. I don't see why the others wouldn't."

"Oh," I said, but it came out as nothing more than a breath of freezing air. "David, um . . . could I . . . talk to you for a sec, please?"

David's face, still bemused, turned serious when he looked back at me.

"Yeah, sure," he said, and came over quickly.

"Are you all right, dear?" Mrs. Wallis said. "You look pale. I'll fix you some oatmeal to go with the hot chocolate. You both look like you could use it."

I nodded and pulled David toward the front door.

"He has a basement!" I whispered fiercely.

"What?"

"It wasn't a pantry," I said, digging my fingers into David's arm. "The pantry I told you I saw, in his house, it's not a pantry, it's a *basement*. A basement with a padlock, David, a *padlock*. What's he got in there? *Who's* he got in there . . . ?"

"Whoa, hold up," David said gently. "So it was a basement, that doesn't prove anything, Pelly. He probably has antiques or tools or something locked up, that's all. Maybe it's a wine cellar, even. Or just an extra room, like this one."

"I've got to go back."

"Pelly! No."

"David, I have to, I have to see—"

"Pel, you're lucky you didn't get caught and hauled off to jail as it is," David said. "C'mon. We've been over this. It was a mistake, a legitimate mistake, that's all."

I'd never convince him. The reality of this crushed my lungs in my chest, heavy chains that cinched me tight.

Maybe David was right, maybe it was a legitimate mistake, but now I had to know for sure. I owed Tara that much. God, maybe I owed myself that much too.

But I would never convince David to go back with me.

Plus I knew that my "evidence" was meaningless to the cops. Tell them what, exactly? That I broke into this old man's home? That he was guilty of putting a lock on his basement door?

I made up my mind.

"You're right," I said. "Of course you're right. It just sounded so plausible, I guess."

David hugged me. "I know," he said. "And I'm sorry."

"It's okay," I said. "I'm going to get some sleep. I'm wiped out."

"No joke," David said. "What about your oatmeal?"

"You can have it. I'm good." I pulled away from him and called toward the kitchen, "Thank you, Mrs. Wallis. I'm going to go upstairs now. Thanks again for everything."

She walked into the living room, drying her hands on a red dish towel. "You're perfectly welcome, dear," she said. "You just let me know if you need anything. Please help yourselves to whatever you find in the kitchen, now, I mean it. Kirk and I will probably be in bed shortly."

"Thanks," I said. I turned back to David and very nearly kissed him good night, but settled for a squeeze of his hand instead. "See you in the morning," I said.

"You want to call your mom again?" he asked. "I need to call mine, let her know . . . well, something. That I won't be back till tomorrow, anyway. How about you?"

"You can text her, I guess," I said. "Tell her I'm . . . trying to spend the night at Alecia's. See if I can do it without freaking."

"Okay. If she texts me back—"

"I'll be asleep. I'll talk to her tomorrow."

"Okay," David said. "See you in the morning."

I walked upstairs, went into the spare room, and closed the door. I sat on the edge of the bed and waited.

Oh, I made up my mind, all right.

Once the house was asleep, I was going to Franklin Rebane's house and rescuing my best friend.

FIFTEEN

It hit me while I paced back and forth across the hardwood floor of the Wallises' spare bedroom that I hadn't heard back from Mom. Had she called David's cell back yet? Would he come up and get me if she did? Maybe he was pacing the basement right now too, debating whether or not to come up here and give me a message or let me talk to her.

The thought of David pacing the basement pretty much destroyed any lingering worries about Mom. David at least could come and go as he pleased. Somehow I doubted the same would be true for Tara, locked up in Rebane's crypt. Whatever trouble I'd be in when I got home, I didn't care.

I wondered how long Tara had been there. All six years? Or had Rebane moved around, throwing people off his scent? I forced myself to stop thinking about it once my mind wandered toward what he might have done, might even be doing this very minute, to my best friend. The sick bastard.

Tara, I'm getting you out of there, I'm on my way, I thought.

An hour later the house was quiet. Time to go.

I shut off the bedroom light and opened the door, sticking my head out. The Wallises kept a nightlight in one corner, and it was plenty bright to see by. I slipped out, closed the door silently, and crept down the stairs. I hadn't noticed any squeaks on the way up, but you never knew.

The coast was clear when I reached the bottom. I went quickly to the front door, unlocked it, and sneaked outside, closing the door behind me. I hated leaving it unlocked like that, but I didn't have much choice. And anyway, I doubted a lot of house burglars were out in the cold checking doorknobs at this time of night, and in a little neighborhood of small homes like this.

It had stopped snowing. Little drifts piled up against bushes, trees, and mailboxes like sugar anthills. I took a deep breath of cold air and began walking in the direction we'd come during the drive, hoping my sense of direction would be enough to get me to Rebane's house.

Doubt crept up my back by the time I reached the intersection of Rosemont and York at the entrance to Rebane's neighborhood. How did I plan to get inside his house? And even if I did get into the house, then there was the padlock on the basement door. How exactly did I plan on breaking that off?

I stopped walking. I should've at least gone through the Wallises' kitchen, grabbed a knife and a flashlight or something. My God, I had nothing, not even a cell phone. Some rescue mission this was going to be.

That's when it hit. The panic. The fear. So familiar it was almost cozy.

My breath shrank in my lungs, making me pant. The cold outside my jeans and hoodie was repelled by waves of an internal freeze, colder by a factor of ten.

I hadn't even brought David. But he wouldn't have come. He didn't believe me. But what if I'd tried a little harder? Maybe I wouldn't be standing out here in the cold, alone, defenseless, and without anything remotely resembling a plan to rescue Tara.

Still. A few hours ago I'd been inside Rebane's house on a whim. I'd beaten my own fear and entered the demon's lair. Maybe I'd have the same luck this time.

"Let's do this," I whispered, and forced myself into the neighborhood.

I walked past his house first. I saw no lights on, but there seemed to be a glow in some of the windows, like ambient light from maybe a nightlight. It wasn't the blue-gray flicker of a TV, anyway.

I followed the street north and turned left. I came to the alley we'd used earlier, and used it to reach Rebane's back wall.

So, first problem. How would I get up and over the wall? I could jump and get my hands on top of it, but there was no way I had the strength to pull myself over without help.

Right?

First time for everything, I guess. I jumped and got my hands on top of the wall, then pulled as hard as I could, pushing the toes of my sneakers into the rough brick for traction.

Made it!

"Holy crap," I whispered to myself. I didn't remember being that proud of myself in a long time.

With my heart beating separately in every organ of my body, I slid to the ground behind the bushes. From there, I could see the source of the ambient light; it came from the kitchen, a yellow tube over the stove. Well, at least I'd be able to see.

Now:

. . . *what* now?

Smash and grab. That seemed the only possibility. First I'd need to see if the kitchen door was open—I mean, it wouldn't cost me anything to at least test it again. But if it was locked as I suspected, one good-size rock would bring that window down. I could unlock the door, rush in, and beat the holy hell out of the padlock . . . no, the latch. The wood around the latch would be the weakest part of the mechanism. I could break that with a rock or a brick, run downstairs, grab Tara, and run back up and out, then race straight for the street, screaming. He wouldn't dare chase us; he'd have to take off, and fast, before the cops got here.

Didn't say it was a *good* plan.

I crawled out of the bushes and stayed on my hands and knees, headed for the car. I used the car as cover to pause and try to catch my breath, which was pretty much impossible at that point. I peered over the hood and scanned the rear windows of the house. Other than the dim glow from the kitchen, the house was still dark. Keeping low, I scurried to the kitchen door and tried the knob. Locked.

I crawled over to the garage and checked the padlock. It lay heavy and cold in my hand, and firmly in place.

Hmm.

As a test, I pulled on one of the double doors. Due to the way the chain was wrapped through the handles, it had some slack, and I was able to open the door a couple of inches. So I tried the second door, and it, too, pulled open a bit.

Just enough room?

I wrapped my scarf around the chain to keep it from rattling. Stretched one arm through the gap in the doors. My shoulder. Gently and slowly, put my head between the doors. I pulled myself through, inch by inch. The red hoodie caught up under my arms, exposing my belly to the cold. After another minute or two of wriggling, I was inside the garage.

Not bad, I thought. For an amateur.

I couldn't see really well at first, but after a minute my eyes were decently adjusted. Windows in the doors allowed additional light, but not much.

I saw nothing surprising. A couple of shovels, flowerpots, sacks of dirt, a pick, rolls of black plastic. I spotted a tool chest and cracked that open. Inside I found a couple rolls of duct tape and the usual assortment of hand tools.

The tape gave me an idea. I had no earthly clue if it would work, but it would beat using a rock.

I pulled a heavy claw hammer, screwdriver, and roll of tape out of the chest and made my way back to the garage doors. I checked through the windows set high on the doors, but nothing outside had changed. I dropped down and squiggled my way out the same way I'd come in. It was easier this time because the doors opened out and offered less resistance than they had coming in.

Pulse thundering in my ears, I moved to the kitchen door and peeked inside. The shade was still raised. He wasn't in the kitchen, and the padlock was still fastened to the basement door. Looking at it practically made me throw up.

Don't quit now, I told myself. *You can be scared all you want after you get Tara out, but please, Pelly, please hold it together and get this done right.*

I knelt down and pulled a few strips of tape from the roll. The kitchen door window was divided into nine small panes. I pressed the tape against the lowest-right corner pane, closest to the knob. I put two layers of tape across the entire pane, then rested the screwdriver's flathead tip against the lowest-right corner.

Hoping, or maybe praying, I raised the hammer and tapped it gently once against the screwdriver handle.

Nothing. I tried it again, a little harder, then again. Finally I heard a small crack.

I released a breath. *It might work, son of a bitch, it just might . . .*

I'm not sure how long I spent chiseling at the pane, but when it let go finally, of course it fell inward and smacked the kitchen linoleum. I gritted my teeth and shrank inside my skin. It hadn't shattered—the tape kept it intact—but glass falling against the ground still sounds like glass falling against the ground.

I leaned back and scanned the upstairs windows. They remained dark. I watched them for a while, to make sure, but saw no sign of life.

I didn't think my heart could beat any faster, but it picked up speed as I reached through the empty pane and twisted the lock. It gave readily under my fingers.

You really are insane, I thought.

"Maybe, but at least I don't talk to myself," I whispered, and almost laughed hysterically. I should probably get back on my meds. If I survived.

Holding the hammer tightly, I opened the kitchen door and put my head just inside, ready to run at the first sign of danger. If Rebane came out, I'd run screaming from the house. I'd make so much noise the whole world would wake up. The police would come. They'd get Tara out and arrest Rebane, send him to prison for a million years.

So why not do that? my little voice screamed at me.

Because cops have to follow rules. Me claiming my best friend was locked in his basement wasn't enough. Plus I was here. I had to get her out myself.

I heard nothing in the house. Just that same odd electric hum.

I moved immediately to the pantry door—I mean, *basement* door—and put the claw end of the hammer between the latch and the door. Just before I began prying, I paused.

Instinct kicked in. I could be wrong, but it would only take a couple seconds. . . .

I slid over to the drawers beneath the counter in the hallway. I pulled one, then another, then a third carefully open. And there they were. A set of keys, several imprinted with the Master Lock logo.

Yes!

I put the hammer in the drawer to free my hands and rushed back to the cellar door, trying each key as quickly as possible. The third one slid in and twisted easily.

Mouth dry, I pulled the lock off and opened the door.

I don't know what I expected as I took that first step onto a splintery wooden stair. A hand to grab my ankle, maybe, or the scent of decayed flesh wafting up to assault me. Neither of these things happened. In fact, I thought I smelled vanilla. The same scent I'd noticed before, only much stronger now.

I descended the stairs slowly, slow enough to count each pore in the gray cinderblock wall on my right. The bricks matched the wall I'd climbed over out back, except for their dismal, unpainted color. The basement seemed surprisingly warm; not as warm as the little hallway behind me but not freezing, either. No lights were on, and I hadn't seen a light switch on the wall anywhere; maybe it was in the hallway and I'd missed it?

As my head cleared the floor level above me, I saw the room's only source of light and likely source of scent. A lit jar candle on a card table in the center of the room flickered slowly, waving back and forth. In its light I saw the room had been sparsely furnished; two folding chairs sat tucked beneath the card table, and a narrow doorway led to a minuscule bathroom that looked unfinished and installed by an amateur do-it-yourselfer. A narrow cot sat pushed into one corner, with a bundle of blankets jumbled on top of it.

That was it. Nothing more.

He had a spare room down here just like the Wallises', and he'd left a candle burning, and that was it.

I would be caught and taken to jail and go to prison for life over a partially finished basement. That's it?

The depth of my stupidity could never be measured.

Time to go. I turned and raced back up to the hallway. I didn't bother with the lock, who cared? I just needed to go before—

"Hi there."

SIXTEEN

I sucked in a breath. Clutched my stomach. Spun around and reeled backward into the kitchen door.

Rebane stood in the doorway between the kitchen and hallway, chin tilted down, looking at me over his glasses. He seemed to take up the entire doorframe. He didn't look like he'd been sleeping.

"If you're looking for drugs," he said, "you chose the wrong house."

I could not speak.

"And I hate to tell you," he went on, not moving, "I don't have a lot of cash lying around."

Absurdly, I shook my head. As if agreeing that he didn't have a lot of cash in the house.

I stuttered, "I'm—I'm—I'm—"

"Breaking and entering," Rebane said. "I suppose I should call the police."

His eyes darted to the pantry door as if just now noticing it was open. His gaze lifted back to me. Thankfully, the kitchen door behind me was still unlocked. I knew I could get out that way. If he didn't grab me first.

Break and enter into a suspected kidnapper's house, my little voice snapped. *You are some critical thinker, Penelope. Nice work.*

"Yes, missy, I'll have to call the police," Rebane said. "Or I could just deal with you myself."

He took one step closer.

At last I screamed. Terror crisscrossed through my limbs like wicked electricity. I spun on one toe, reaching for the kitchen doorknob. In the next moment his full weight crashed against me. Pressing me into the door.

"No you don't," he grunted.

I felt his hands on me, everywhere at once, tentacles. Opened my mouth to scream. One of those tentacles slithered over my face. He yanked the basement door wide open, turned, and shoved.

I flew down the steps. Landed midway down the staircase.

"Be right back," Rebane called. He slammed the door shut. I heard the padlock click home.

I pulled myself down the stairs on quaking limbs until I reached the cold concrete floor. Curled up in a ball. Shook. Gasped. Babbled.

A ghost rose in the far corner of the room.

My hands flew automatically to my mouth to stifle the cry of shock. I only caught half of it.

The figure on the cot shot up, staring at me, clearly as frightened as I was.

Tara.

"Hello?" she said fearfully.

She'd been covered by dull blankets, a vague lump in the flickering candlelight. That's why I hadn't seen her before. I stood up and threw myself onto the cot, hugging her close in both arms.

"Tara!" I whispered, as joy, relief, terror, love, and hate all swirled through me in a vortex. I couldn't think.

"Who are you?" Tara whispered back. She wasn't hugging me.

"It's me, it's Pelly!" I said, pulling away and holding her by the shoulders. "From the coffee shop, from the *mall*, Tara, it's *me*."

Tara scooted back from me, clinging to the rough gray wall. In the candlelight her features were shadowed and distorted. She wore a white T-shirt, the blankets now covering her from the waist down. Something clanked as she moved.

"My name's not Tara," she said.

She's so far gone, I thought. *She has no idea who she even is.*

"Tara, listen, we're going to get you out of here," I said. "I—I—I don't know how yet, but I'm getting you—"

"My name isn't Tara," the girl said. "It's Jody."

I froze. Despite the urgency of our predicament, I couldn't move.

"Rebane," I blurted. "Rebane said your name was Leslie in the coffee shop. I knew he was lying, but . . ."

"I know," the girl said. "Leslie, that's what he calls me. I think that's what he called all of them. But my name is Jody O'Malley. Why do you keep calling me Tara? Who *are* you?"

She stared at me across that dim candlelight. In that moment, I saw it. Saw what I should've seen in the Hole in the Wall.

"Oh my God," I whispered. Tried not to get sick all over myself as the truth of the situation sank into my skin, saturated my bones.

Jody's eyes were blue.

Just as blue in this godforsaken basement hellhole as they'd been in the café.

Tara's were brown.

Just like Mrs. Jacobs, just like Mr. Jacobs, just like her older sister, Carla.

Brown eyes.

How could you forget that, you idiot? Don't go putting this on your college apps, okay? My gloved fingers felt automatically for my rubber band to snap against my wrist. Couldn't find it. Tore off the gloves, threw them aside.

"Can you really get me out of here?" Tara—Jody—asked.

"I . . . I don't know . . ."

She flung off the blankets and I gasped. Jody was naked other than the T-shirt. A sinister, heavy shackle bound one of her thin ankles to a weighty chain that snaked off one edge of the cot. I didn't have to look beneath the bed to know with utter certainty that the end of the chain was attached to the cinderblock wall or the concrete floor.

The first words I could make come out of my mouth were simply, "My god."

As she moved, her shirt slipped a bit. I was able to see her neck and shoulder. There was that small mole on her neck, just as I'd seen last week. But so much higher. Near her ear, not lower near the shoulder like Tara's. Only about three or four inches of difference, and yet all the difference in the world.

Some detective you are, Penelope, the voice in my head told me. *You're a champion. You couldn't piece this together back in the café? Brilliant.*

And what about the age-enhanced photos? I must've really only seen what I wanted. Needed.

"How'd you get in?" Jody said. "Do you have a key? Where is he?"

"I don't know, I think so, I . . . keys . . . the keys are upstairs, I left them."

Upstairs, the basement door opened, then slammed shut.

We clutched each other as ponderous footsteps descended the stairs. As if in slow motion, Rebane appeared, carrying a wooden cane in both hands.

"Well, well," he said. "My two little birds. What are we going to do about this, hmm?"

And he laughed.

I wish I could say I sprang into action. That I grabbed Jody's chain and whirled it over my head like some barbaric Wonder Woman, slamming it into Rebane's head and making our escape.

I wish I could say I *moved*. Attempted to do something.

I didn't.

I was as frozen on that cot as I'd been earlier in Rebane's living room. Whether it was his power or my weakness, I don't know. I knew this feeling, knew it well, like my own skin. It was panic, it was fear, it was everything that had been wrong with me since Tara disappeared. Like gravity had multiplied exponentially beneath me, keeping me rooted to this cot, just as it had rooted me to the doorway of my house before school. I couldn't move then, and I couldn't move now.

Why—why on earth had I thought I had what it took to rescue Tara?

"Before you make too many plans," Rebane said, leaning against the stair railing, "you'll want to take special note of the fact that the lock on this side of the door is a combination. Anything happens to me down here, and we'll be going through it together for a very long time."

Bastard. Genius bastard. I hadn't even seen the other lock on this side of the door.

"S-someone will notice you're gone," I said. "Come looking for you."

"Then by all means," Rebane said. "Try it."

So much for that idea. His words acted like ice in my lungs.

Rebane smiled as he watched horror spread across my face. "You must be the little whatsit that busted in earlier tonight. I knew something wasn't right when I got home. Didn't think you'd be back. But now that you're here with Leslie—"

"*Jody!*" she screamed. "*My name is Jody, you asshole!*"

Rebane clucked his tongue and shook his head in mocking disappointment.

"Now, Les," he said, "you know what that kind of language calls for in this house, right?"

He may as well have flipped a switch. The fight in Jody's voice and limbs gushed out. She sank onto the mattress like a deflated balloon. My mind filled with images of what his threat implied. Things I could barely fathom. Atrocities, abuse, torture . . .

"What did you do to her?" I heard myself saying as Jody curled up on the thin, hard mattress.

Rebane took slow, practiced steps toward me, squeezing the cane in his fingers.

"Oh, about the same's I'm gonna do to you," he said. "Anybody even know you're here, missy?"

I swallowed hard. Said nothing.

"Didn't think so," Rebane said. He paused, scrutinizing me more closely. "What the—" he said, and didn't come any closer. "I know you. I've seen you before. Where?"

I shook my head. As if that would keep him from remembering.

"Yes, I have," Rebane said carefully, like he was giving himself time to let the memory come to him. "Recently. A store, maybe. That coffee shop!"

I cringed.

"That's right," he went on as his greasy, leering smile spread like a tumor across his face. "The cute little barista. Well, well, well. What brings you here, hmm?"

I forced myself not to look at Jody, but it didn't matter. He put the pieces together.

"That's right," he said. "You thought you knew my little Leslie. Except you don't, do you."

I shook my head again. It made Rebane laugh.

"Don't suppose it matters now," he said. "You're here. With me."

Jody released a dismal whimper.

"Now, honestly, missy, you and I both know that you had a little thing for me. I felt it back at your coffee shop. So this really won't be such a bad thing. You wanted it, you're getting it. Think about all the fun we're going to have over the next few days."

I felt a scream building in my chest, but it wouldn't come out.

"Or weeks," Rebane added as he took another step closer.

"Or months.

"Or . . . well. You do the math."

"Please," I wheezed. "Please just let us go."

"I was about through with Leslie, anyway," Rebane went

on. "You'll do for a bit. But just a bit. You're spoiled. I can smell it on you. Broken and spoiled."

I almost puked. I didn't know what he was talking about. And it didn't matter.

Franklin Rebane was crazy.

"You think I'm crazy, don't you?" Rebane said, and when he did, a sick moan came out of my mouth. He could read my mind.

"Well, unfortunately for you, I'm not," Rebane said. It didn't convince me.

"Not at all," he said. "Oh, I'll admit, I am going to do some pretty depraved things to you down here. Isn't that right, Leslie?"

Jody whimpered again, closing her eyes and turning away from him as if bracing herself. Dear God, what had he—

"Yep, that much is certain," Rebane went on. And licked his lips.

"But I'm not crazy. And frankly, that's probably what should worry you the most. See, you just happen to be here. You came here all under your own steam. I don't think a little cuss like you will be missed. And down here I can do whatever I want. Whenever I want. For as long as I want. Just you, and me, and my imagination. Thrilling, isn't it? So, am I crazy? Nope."

"People know I'm here!" I said.

"Really? Who?"

"My-my-my mom. My mom knows. She'll call the police, and—and—and—"

"Mm-hmm," Rebane said.

"I've been to the police. If I go missing, they'll come here first, they'll look for me right here!"

Rebane gave me a pitying look. "Even if that's true," he said, "it just means I can't keep you around for quite so long."

"I'm sorry," I blurted. "I'm so sorry, I shouldn't have bothered you, you can let us both go and—"

"You should stop talking," Rebane said. "You'll need your strength. It's a bit late in the evening, I suppose, but what's say we get started?"

Started. The word tumbled between my ears like a canyon echo. *Started. Started . . .*

Just as Rebane was about to close in on me, I heard a voice of angels from upstairs. Distant, muted. But there.

"Pelly!"

"David!" I shrieked.

Like some elderly Jedi, Rebane backhanded me with the cane against my temple, sending me against the wall, then toppling off the bed. I tried to rescrew my eyeballs back into their correct sockets as Rebane bolted up the stairs.

I groaned David's name. At least I was conscious. I thought I saw Jody folding her knees against her chest and covering her head with both hands.

Rebane hadn't lost his genius. He rushed up the stairs and pounded on the basement door, shouting, "We're in here! He locked us in here!"

It was so absurd it was brilliant. Exactly the kind of lie that would throw a normal person off balance.

"If you pull and I push, I think we can get the door to open," Rebane went on.

"David . . . ," I said, trying to warn him, but I was still too groggy from the blow to my head to project my voice.

The next few moments went by at the speed of fear.

Dim light flooded the stairwell from the hallway. I heard muttering, then flesh meeting flesh. A grunt, and a sickening series of thunks as David tumbled down the stairs and came to rest at the bottom, not moving.

See, Penelope? You see what you did? You killed him.

With a cry that tore my lungs apart, I pushed myself up and raced for the stairs, leaping over David's prone body. I bounded up the steps two at a time, using the handrail to propel me. Rebane was just turning in the doorway, the outer padlock in his hand.

He tried to slam the door on me. I knew if he did, our fates were sealed.

I heard him grumble something profane as he shoved a hand into my face. The blow cranked my neck back and made me lose my vision for a split second. Just long enough for Rebane to slam the door, trapping me inside the basement. A moment later I heard the outer lock click into place.

I lifted my fists to pound on the door, but stopped. I knew it wouldn't do any good. Plus there was David to think about.

I ran back down the stairs. David, thankfully, was starting to pull himself into a sitting position.

"David!" I said, and knelt down beside him. "Are you okay?"

"Uh . . . ," David said, his eyes half-closed. "Maybe?"

"We've got to get out of here," I said.

"You can't," Jody said, still curled up on the cot. "He's gonna kill us all."

SEVENTEEN

"What do you mean?" I blurted, as if Jody had been speaking a foreign language.

"He won't keep us all down here alive," Jody said listlessly. "He can't afford it. We'd be too much trouble. He'll kill him"—she waved weakly toward David, who glanced up and winced—"and then one of us. Probably me. You're young. Who is *this* guy, anyway?"

"A friend. Doesn't matter, we're getting out of here," I said, trying to sound determined. Instead I sounded like a mouse in a trap.

"Help me up," David groaned.

"Maybe you shouldn't move," I said. "Your head's bleeding."

David touched the line of blood running down his face and held his fingers up to his eyes. "It is dark in here, right?" he asked. "It's not just me?"

"There's just the candle, it's the only light," I said. I turned to Jody. "Isn't there another light in here somewhere?"

She shook her head. "The bathroom isn't wired, and the ceiling bulb is controlled in the kitchen," she said. "He only turns it on when he . . . he likes to *see* what—"

"Stop, stop," I said, shutting my eyes for a second. I didn't want to know.

David began standing again. I tried to keep him down. "Don't," I said. "You might have a concussion or something."

"Doesn't matter," David said, using the wall to help himself up. "We have to get out."

"Where's your phone?"

"By the kitchen door," David said. "Knocked it outta my hands."

Shit.

I snapped my rubber band against my wrist to sort my thoughts into a logical order. Went to the cot and took Jody by the shoulders.

"Jody," I said. "Is there any, *any* other way out of here? Or any way we can surprise him?"

Jody shook her head. Pretty much what I'd expected. The basement had no windows, no other doors. It was exactly what I'd imagine an underground concrete bunker to be: four walls, the little homemade doorless bathroom nook, and wooden steps up to the door in the kitchen. Other than the table and cot, there was no furniture. The only real hiding place was under the stairs, but it wasn't like one of us could go there and surprise him.

David pointed to the candle. "What if we burn it down?"

"He'll leave us here," Jody said. "Let us burn."

"Does he have a gun?" I said. "Have you ever seen one?"

"Yes," Jody said. "I've seen it. A pistol."

"That's not a good start," David said, wincing.

The door opened.

Instinctively I drew back against the far wall, standing beside the cot. David backed up too, as if to shield me and Jody.

We heard Rebane messing with the combination padlock. When it clicked into place, my stomach deflated. He took the steps one at a time as if making sure we weren't going to jump him.

My limbs froze as I saw a silvery revolver dangling from Rebane's hand. Grim in the shadows cast by the candle, the gun seemed impossibly huge.

"Yooo hoooo," Rebane sang softly. "Is everybody here?"

I found myself wishing for the days when "fear" meant not wanting to go to school, or to stay inside all day. I could've laughed. That wasn't fear. This. This was the real thing, real terror, real certainty that I was going to die. I heard myself chanting, *I'm sorry, I'm sorry, I'm sorry*, not knowing if it was out loud or only in my head.

Rebane reached the floor and turned toward us, carrying the pistol at thigh level.

"Leslie?" Rebane said. "You want to go first?"

"They'll hear it," David said. His voice was desperate. "Someone'll hear the shot, and they'll come—"

"Leslie?" Rebane said. "Is that true? Will someone hear the shots?"

He'd used the plural. Jody shook her head dismally.

"No," Rebane said. "They won't. They've never heard anything from down here. Isn't that right, Leslie?"

Someone said, "Leave her alone."

Rebane tilted his head. He stared at me, his face incredulous in the candlelight.

I'd said it.

"What?" he grunted.

I pushed past David. He whispered my name. I ignored it.

I got mad.

I got mad at whoever took Tara, some son of a bitch just like Rebane. I got mad at myself for letting the fear paralyze me. I was sure as hell mad at Rebane for terrorizing this girl, and for doing the same to me and David.

In the last few seconds of my life, I was free.

"I said leave her alone!"

Rebane blinked. Frowned. Then smiled. "Oh, missy," he said. "I'm so sad we won't be able to have any fun before I plant you. But them's the breaks."

He took a step toward me. Raised the gun to my face. I felt like I could see down the entire length of that awful cylinder to the shell beyond, primed and ready to tear my head off my shoulders.

Then Rebane shifted his aim and pulled the trigger. The room exploded, and I fell backward into Jody on the cot.

Audible pain ricocheted down the base of my skull, through my spine, and into my knees. Ten pounds of wet sand poured into each ear, heavy and damp. My ribs vibrated like a xylophone, quaking and threatening to puncture my lungs. Smoke congested the air, choking me.

I screamed, *What happened?* but the sound only echoed at the back of my throat. It was like talking underwater, heavy and muted.

I ran my hands down my body and back up. Everything was in place, as far as I could tell. I was alive.

David fell.

He dropped to the concrete floor in a heap, like his bones had been yanked out of his skin. I shouted his name, but stopped after that because the sensation of speaking while deaf made my eyes water. Jody whimpered behind me while I faced up to Rebane again. The freedom I'd enjoyed for all of three seconds was gone.

"And now you," he said, and swung the pistol toward me.

Thoughtless, my mind blank, I took my rubber band off my wrist and pulled it against my right index finger, stretch-ing it back past my wrist using my left hand. I pointed it at Rebane's face and let it go.

The band snapped against his cheek. Rebane's face wrinkled up, and he gave a surprised squealing sound.

Then he grinned. Carnivorous.

"All right," he said in a low voice. "A little fight in you. I like that. I like that. C'mere."

He tucked the pistol into his back pocket and lunged. Before I could react, he was on top of me. Pinning me against Jody, the cot, and the wall. In seconds he was straddling me, keeping my legs pinned between his own, one calloused hand around my throat. My eyes rolled crazily, my breath cut off.

Both my hands automatically flung to his arm and pulled, tore, grabbed. I pried at his wrist with both hands, wishing I had longer nails. He just grinned and continued muttering profane things, things he had done to Jody, things he was going to do to me, all my worst nightmares growing and taking awful, tangible shape as his other hand touched me, scraped at me, like some rabid beast that should be put down—

Whether it was from lack of oxygen, or that I'd remembered more of what David had said—I stopped struggling. Let myself go limp. *Don't try to beat his strength.*

"Yeah," Rebane grunted. "That's it. Yeah. Just relax. Just relax, baby."

My hands fell to my sides and my eyes closed.

That's when I felt it. A hard square tucked into the coin pocket of my jeans.

My pillbox.

Rebane didn't release me, but his grip on my neck loosened ever so slightly. I could breathe again. Barely. My heart rampaged in my chest. My breaths were short, shallow, scarcely enough to live.

Rebane fumbled at his waist. With his belt. The sound of the buckle tinkled in my ears, making them want to bleed. I used my right hand to dig into my coin pocket.

"Almost there," Rebane whispered. "Almost there, baby."

Pulled the pillbox out. Flicked it open. With the ease of years of practice, flipped my cutter into my fingers.

"Yeah," Rebane said. "Yeah, here we *GAAAAH!*"

Mustering what remained of my strength, I reached up and dragged the blade across his wrist as hard as I could.

Blood spilled from the wound. Rebane roared and fell backward, his pants down around his thighs. I heard the pistol clatter to the floor. His right hand immediately went to his left wrist, trying to stop the blood.

Screaming, I leaped at him. Slashed at his face. Found skin. Tore the blade down his cheek, opening another gushing wound.

"You rotten bitch!" he roared. "I'm gonna—"

I rolled off the cot. My blade dropped. I scooped the gun into numb hands and pulled the trigger.

Deafness. A total vacuum. Everything in slow motion.

Rebane froze, eyes bulging in the dull candlelight. He clutched his belly. Curled over. Fell to the floor.

He was still breathing.

Not for long.

I shuffled on my knees over to him and shoved the barrel of the gun to his head. Said things, I don't know what. I couldn't hear myself. Began to squeeze that trigger to end him, make him pay.

. . . *eeeee* . . .

I paused.

. . . ellie . . .

A distant groan. I turned.

David, on his side, one hand pressed against his collarbone, reached out to me with his other hand. My hearing cleared up and I heard him saying my name.

"Pelly . . ."

Still alive, my voice said. *He's still alive, got to get out of here, got to . . .*

I ran up the stairs. The door was locked with a round combo lock, just as Rebane had said. But I still had his gun.

Wincing against the noise and recoil, I shot two bullets into the door around the latch, like I'd planned to do with the hammer earlier that night. It worked. The wood splintered out, and I managed to bash the door the rest of the way open.

I needed a phone. But what I found first were the keys. Rebane had unlocked the padlock, and tossed it and the key ring on the hallway counter. I grabbed them and rushed back downstairs. After a few tries I unlocked Jody's chain. She stumbled off the cot and climbed up the stairs on her hands and feet like it was a ladder. I dragged the shackle over to Rebane's feet, trying to ignore the blood spreading across his shirt. I quickly locked his ankle into the shackle.

"That's how it feels," I said.

Then I slid over to David. "Can you move?"

"Not good," he moaned.

"You have to," I said. "Come on."

Somehow I got him to his feet, and we climbed out of the basement. In the kitchen hallway David lost his footing, and he dropped to the floor.

I leaned down to haul him back up, but he shook his head. "Cops," he grunted. "Hurry. Ambulance."

I spun around, looking for David's phone. Nothing here. Ran into the kitchen. Found Jody already on a black wall-mounted telephone. Giving directions.

"They're coming," she said.

"Okay," I said. "Okay."

And don't remember much after that.

EIGHTEEN

When I came to, Jody was beside me. She helped me sit up and lean against one kitchen wall.

"Are you all right?" she asked.

"Think so," I said. "David . . ."

"He's still in the hall, he's alive," she said. "The cops are on their way. You blacked out, I think."

I nodded. My lungs seemed to take up my entire torso. Everything inside me felt painfully inflated and raw.

Jody stood up and leaned against the doorway leading to the living room, looking around and blinking as if it were a sunny day and she was coming out of a cave, except it was still night and there were only two lamps lit. She'd wrapped a blanket around her waist.

"How long?" I whispered. "How long have you been down there?"

Without turning, Jody said, "Two years. I think."

"You did say 'Help me,' right?" I said. "At the coffee shop the other day?"

"Yes. I didn't think you would, though. No one has before."

"Before? It wasn't the first time? Why did he take you out there?"

Her narrow shoulders shrugged up. In the distance I heard sirens.

"Part of his fantasy, his power trip," she said. "I think it made him feel strong. He took me to restaurants sometimes, or the store. I wanted to scream, but . . ."

Something about her words formed another question for me. "Jody? How old are you?"

"Seventeen now, I think. Maybe eighteen." At last she turned, and I saw both premature age and incredible youth in her face. "Who is Tara?"

"A friend," I said as red flashing lights penetrated the curtains of the picture window. "Just a friend I haven't seen in a long time."

"Your name's . . . Pelly?" Jody asked.

"It's short for Penelope. Yeah."

"Thanks for saving my life, Penelope."

I wanted to put a hand on her shoulder, or hug her, or something—but couldn't stand. "You're welcome," I said, feeling inadequate.

The front door crashed open, making us both jump. Two

cops lunged into the room, guns clasped in their hands, pointed at the floor.

"He's in the basement," Jody told the cop. "He's not going anywhere. He's chained to the wall."

"My boyfriend's shot," I said weakly, not aware I'd even used that particular word until a lot later. "He needs help."

I don't know how much time passed after that. I saw paramedics coming for David and wheeling him out on a stretcher. I called to him, but the EMTs said they needed to get him out. Then another set of paramedics got Rebane out of the basement and onto another gurney. He was not conscious.

Jody and I were both led to a third ambulance. We answered ten thousand questions, half from the EMTs, half from uniformed cops. The next thing I knew, we were in the small Canyon City hospital being looked over by doctors.

I know that at some point my mother was called. I know that at some point a nurse told me David would be fine. I know that someone else said they thought Rebane would live. I know that Jody got whisked away by some cops, and we didn't even say good-bye to each other.

And I know I fell asleep for what turned out to be almost twenty-four hours.

NINETEEN

I became a minor celebrity for the second time in my life.

When Tara had disappeared, I'd been too young to be interviewed for *Abducted*, the TV show, but not anymore. I got phone call after phone call from TV stations asking for interviews. First they were calling me at the Hole in the Wall, which ultimately made me quit. Eli and the rest of the staff didn't need to be bombarded by this stuff.

By the time I got home, the media people—newspapers, websites, TV shows, you name it—had tracked down my address and even my mom's cell phone number. Surprisingly, Mom took it in stride, and I couldn't help but admire the way she really told off some of the reporters.

"She'll let you know when she's ready," she'd say. "Until then, we ask that you respect her privacy."

But during one particularly obnoxious call she ended with,

"So screw you and the horse you rode in on!" which made us both laugh so hard we almost fell to the ground.

I hadn't laughed with my mom in a long time.

Mom had come up to Canyon City with Jeffrey to pick me up from the police station. She hugged me so tight I thought she'd snap one of my ribs. She kept chanting, "I'm sorry, Penelope, I'm so sorry, I'm sorry," over and over in my ear.

Jeffrey thought I was the ultimate badass, which I kind of enjoyed. Dad rushed home for the first time ever, and hugged me for so long it hurt my neck. I didn't mind so much.

A month after I returned from Canyon City, I woke up and moseyed into the kitchen for breakfast. Freshly made waffles, melting butter, and hot coffee made for an excellent first-thing-in-the-morning aroma.

"Morning," I said as I walked into the kitchen. I plopped down beside Mom and reached for the carafe of orange juice to chase away my morning mouth. Jeffrey was in his room getting ready for school.

"Morning, Pelly," Mom said, but was frowning with one hand over her mouth. "They haven't told you yet, have they?"

"Who told me what?"

"The police found three bodies buried in his backyard," she said. She didn't have to clarify who she was referring to. "Three girls. They were beneath a bed of flowers. Ugh! What an awful human being."

The juice curdled in my mouth.

The flower garden. Such pretty flowers. Without asking, I knew one of them was named Leslie.

I felt chains twisting around my ribs, squeezing the air out of me. My heart began knocking from the inside, *bam! bam! bam!* Let me *out . . .*

No, I thought. *Stop. You are safe. You are safe.*

I finished my juice and wiped my mouth. "No," I said. My voice came out higher than normal. "They hadn't told me that. Was one of them . . . I mean, Tara wasn't . . . ?"

"No," Mom said, touching my hand. "Not Tara."

I nodded. I didn't think so either. Had to ask.

"There's an article here, if you want to read it," Mom went on. "But I don't suppose you'd want that."

"No," I said. The invisible chains around my body began to relax and drift away. "Not today, anyway. I'm a little distracted."

Mom reached for my hand and squeezed it. "I'd imagine so." With her free hand Mom brushed at her cheeks. "I'm so glad you're safe, Pel."

Didn't know what to say to that, so I just squeezed her hand back.

Mom sniffed and coughed, then got up with her empty plate and put it in the sink. "You have an appointment later today, remember."

"Four o'clock, yeah, I know."

"How's, um . . . how's that going?"

She hadn't brought up Dr. Carpenter since I started going

back, which I appreciated. But I also appreciated that she was asking.

"Good," I said after swallowing a mouthful of waffles. "She said I'm making progress. I don't know what that means, though. Maybe I'll ask her today."

Mom smiled and pulled me over to her so she could kiss my head and ruffle my hair.

Jeffrey bounded into the kitchen with his usual enthusiasm. He gave me a hug from behind, nearly choking me out.

"Hey, sis!" he cried in my ear.

"Hey, Jeffrey," I said, reaching behind me and tickling his ribs.

Jeffrey shot away from my fingers and went straight for the fridge. "You gonna see David today?"

"You bet," I said. "He's picking me up in a few minutes."

"So then after school can he come over and play games?"

"I'll ask him," I said. "But probably, yeah."

"Awesome!"

I smiled at my little brother as he poured himself juice. "Little" didn't seem to fit anymore. He was almost as tall as I was now, and probably going to get a lot taller.

"You're a crazy little nut factory, you know that?" I said as he sat at the table.

"Look who's talking!" Jeffrey said.

"Exactly. You're a nut factory because you make me nuts. Get it?"

My brother rolled his eyes. And I laughed.

David pulled up to the sidewalk a few minutes after Mom

and Jeffrey left. I went out to meet him, locking our door behind me. I climbed into the truck and kissed him.

"Morning, sunshine," David said. "Mint mocha?"

He passed me the white cup with the Hole in the Wall logo on it.

"You are a god among men," I said. "Thanks."

"So?" David asked, pulling away from the curb. "How you feeling about today?"

"Nervous," I said. "Hey, I talked to Jody last night."

"Whoa, no kidding?" David said. "She call you?"

"Yeah. It was surreal. She's on medication, and getting therapy, so we sort of bonded over that."

David snickered, and so did I.

"I know, right?" I said. "And I asked her why she never tried to escape."

"She never did?" David asked.

"No. She said it was like Stockholm syndrome or something. Like she'd started depending on him. She said she was afraid she'd even started to enjoy it."

"Wow," David said softly.

I nodded. I knew what Jody'd meant, to some degree. I thought about the psych hospital I'd lived in. How it had gotten so comfortable. So easy after a while. Easier than dealing with the real world.

I didn't tell David this part, but on the phone Jody had asked me, *Do you think you can be addicted to something that makes you feel awful? Even when you know it's wrong, that it's not good for you? I don't mean drugs. I mean people. Or thoughts.*

Or memories, I'd said. *Yeah. I do.*

"Anyway, she just wanted to say thanks again and all that," I went on to David as he made a slow left turn.

"Very cool," David said. "I'm glad you got a chance to talk to her."

"Me too," I said.

Up ahead I saw one of the few things that still scared me. My right hand reached for my left, searching instinctively for my rubber band. It wasn't there. Hadn't been there, in fact, since I fired my last one at Rebane. The memory almost made me laugh. But—not quite.

I took a deep breath through my nose and exhaled slowly from my mouth, the way David had been showing me. It worked. My thoughts settled into a jumbled pile instead of zipping around like little angry bumblebees. It was a start.

David pulled into a large parking lot and, after jockeying a bit, managed to find a space somewhere in the middle. The lot was packed, and people streamed toward the building in the chilly air.

"Ready?" David asked, turning off the engine.

"No," I said.

"What's up?"

"*What's up?* I'm scared to death, that's what's up."

He twisted his mouth around a couple times. "Scared, or afraid?"

"I just said I was scared. You don't listen so well, Harowitz."

"That's true," he said, grinning. "What I'm saying is that 'scared' is an adrenaline dump. It's that fight-or-flight thing. Scared helps keep you alive. Afraid is . . . it's a lifestyle. It's a slow burn, always on. So you're scared, or you're afraid?"

I'd never thought about distinguishing between the two. Terrified, horrified, afraid, fearful, scared—synonymous to me. But I saw his point. I didn't answer right away.

"Okay," I said. "Scared, then."

"That's good," David said. "I mean, good that you're not afraid."

"I just don't want to go in there," I said, gazing at the monumental building beyond my passenger-side window.

"Me either," David said. "And I'll take you home right now if you want. But then you'd have to have lunch all by yourself. And that would suck for me."

He smiled. It settled my nerves just a bit.

"They're going to stare," I said.

"Probably."

"Gee, thanks."

"Lying to you won't help. Yes, they'll stare. Some of them. But honestly, a lot won't. And the ones that do, so what?"

"Will you beat them up for me if they do?"

"Excuse me, I just got my stitches out from being *shot*," David said with faux indignation. His wound had been ugly but not bad. He'd been able to come home after a few days in the Canyon City hospital.

"And besides," he went on, "if anyone in this car can kick

someone's ass, it's you. Don't tell me you forgot what you can do when someone makes you mad. I mean, I wouldn't cross you, and I know wing chun."

"And tap," I said.

"Yes, *and* tap."

Finally I smiled back at him. Couldn't help it. Then my calves burned, aching for relief, to bleed, to drain the pressure and stress off what I had to do next. What I'd *chosen* to do next. But I couldn't cut now. Not now, and not here. Maybe when I got home.

And maybe not even then. David knew about the cuts, and now so did my family; I'd had to explain why and how I came to have a razor blade in my pocket that awful night. I'd told Dr. Carpenter right away too, when I went back for my first appointment. She didn't act surprised, and she didn't tell me to stop. She just asked if I wanted to work on stopping. And I said yes.

I was already five days in, so. That was something.

"Is there a smoking section?" I asked.

"No, but I know the people who know where you can get away with it. I'll introduce you." He smirked. "I got a guy."

"Nice."

"You're still going to quit, right?"

"Someday."

"It's a lot easier to kiss you when you haven't been smoking. Just, you know. FYI."

"Someday *soon*," I corrected.

"Cool," David said. And kissed me. I hadn't smoked yet that morning. "Ready to go?"

I nodded, and we climbed out of his truck. As I expected, even before we reached the sidewalk, a few people turned their heads to look at me. Or maybe they were looking at us. Meaning, *as* an "us." I don't know. But a few of them smiled. So that wasn't so bad. One guy even flexed a fist and gave me an approving scowl.

I took David's hand in mine. He looked down at them entwined, then up at me. He grinned, and bobbed his head toward the imposing redbrick building.

"You got this, you know," he said as a bell rang. "You can do it."

"Yeah," I said. "I got this."

I wished, of course, that Tara was on my other side. I wondered what she'd think of David. I wondered if she was still out there, like Jody had been, or if something worse had happened. If there was any chance I'd see her again.

And I wondered if I'd ever stop wondering. Probably not. That was okay. I still had to do this part. I knew she'd want that.

Hand in hand with David, I walked into school.

Turn the page for a peek at Tom Leveen's RANDOM.

Who's the real victim?

Late at night Tori receives a random phone call. It's a wrong number. But the caller seems to want to talk, so she stays on the line.

He asks for a single thing—one reason not to kill himself.

The request plunges her into confusion. Because if this random caller actually does what he plans, he'll be the *second* person connected to Tori to take his own life. And the first just might land her in jail. After her Facebook page became Exhibit A in a tragic national news story about cyberbullying, Tori can't help but think the caller is a fraud. But what if he's not? Her words alone may hold the power of life or death.

With the clock ticking, Tori has little time to save a stranger—and maybe redeem herself—leading to a startling conclusion that changes everything. . . .

ONE

They've been pounding on the front door for more than an hour, which is exactly how long it took for Dad to make his famous garlic mashed potatoes. He'd slammed the masher down time after time, *BAM! BAM! BAM!* with his lips drawn tight as Mom took measured steps between the stove and sink while making Italian meat loaf.

It feels like a last meal.

"I just want to ask a few questions, Victoria!" this one reporter keeps shouting through our closed door. Her name is Allison Summers. I've never met her face-to-face, still don't know what she looks like, but I know what she thinks of me, and what she made the rest of the world think of me. So she can stay out there and melt in the rain like the witch she is, for all I care.

None of us inside speaks. We just do our routine jobs,

but without saying a word. Normally Mom would be singing R.E.M. singles, or Dad would be reciting a stand-up routine from some dead comedian, or my brother, Jack, and I would be debating about whether or not Olympic athletes were "superhuman."

Tonight: a vast silence, like standing in an empty gymnasium.

Jack, in particular, makes it a point to not even look at me. I'm not used to this treatment from my older brother yet, even though he's been doing it for weeks. Mom and Dad are letting him do it too. That doesn't make me feel any better.

"Jack, where's the green napkins?" I ask as he pulls down plates.

He doesn't even point. I can see his jaw muscles working as he clenches his teeth, making his deep, pitted acne scars look like pulsing lunar craters. Jack had cystic acne all through high school, and people always called him all kinds of terrible names, even up till he graduated last year. Krakatoa, Pus Factory. Even Zit Face.

I never called him anything. He doesn't seem to remember that.

"Please, Miss Hershberger, this might be your only chance to set the story straight," Allison-the-reporter calls, pound-pound-pounding on the door some more.

"Check the other cabinet for the napkins, Tori," Mom says. She tries to make it casual, as if there aren't a bunch of report-ers on our lawn in a light spring rain, but her voice is tight and strained.

So I check the other cabinet, and there are the green napkins, just where I knew they'd be. I'd asked only to see if maybe Jack would forget he wasn't talking to me and say something.

With Dad's potatoes done finally, we sit down around our small dining room table just off the kitchen. It's more of a nook than a room. We eat here six nights a week. Even now. Mom tries to smile at me as she gestures to the meat loaf, urging me to serve myself first.

"Victoria?" Allison Summers calls. "I'm on deadline. I'm filing a story tonight whether you talk to me or not, so you might want to think about telling people your side of things."

Another voice, male, shouts, "Have you decided on a plea?"

Dad's chair flips backward when he stands up. My stomach contracts and pulls me taut against my chair, and Mom drops a fork. Jack doesn't move, just sits there staring at his empty plate.

Dad races to the front door. I hear him fling it open.

"Get off my property!" Dad shouts. "Now! Every single last one of you, out!"

"Mr. Hershberger, I just want—"

"Out! I'll call the police on all of you, get out!"

"Mr. Hersh—"

"*Go!*" Dad roars, throwing a giant mother-F-bomb out with it. "You're nothing but a bunch of bloodsucking vultures! Get off my property and leave my family alone!"

I've never heard Dad swear before. Or yell. He's a grumbler, not a screamer.

"Thought we were supposed to ignore them," Jack whispers, not lifting his eyes.

"Easy for Mr. Halpern to say," Mom says, her voice wrenching a bit tighter. "He's probably having a quiet dinner."

I hear muttering at the front door, and a moment later it slams shut. Instead of coming back to the table, though, Dad stalks past us and goes down the hall and into he and Mom's bedroom. Another slammed door twists my stomach again.

At least the knocking has stopped. After a few more minutes I hear a couple of car engines start up and drive away from the front of our house.

I let out a breath I didn't know I'd been holding. Jack takes his napkin from his lap and tosses it on the empty plate.

"Are you even sorry?" he says.

I look up at him, blinking. These are the first words Jack's spoken to me in weeks. So of course I screw it right up.

"What kind of question is that?"

"A simple kind," Jack snaps. "Just answer it. Are you?"

"Jack," Mom says, "maybe now isn't—"

I'm too angry to let her even finish. I shout back at him, "Of course I am, Jack! God!"

Mom says, "Kids, please . . ."

Jack leans over the table, resting his forearms on the top. "Sorry you did it, or sorry you're in trouble?"

"What's the difference?"

Jack snorts and pushes his chair back. He stands up, takes one step, stops.

"God, Vic," he says. "I don't even recognize you anymore."

I try to come up with something to shoot back and come up empty. Plus, I kind of know what he means. I haven't *felt* much like myself.

"Jack," Mom says again.

"I've got homework," he says. "Might as well do some while I'm still enrolled."

"It'll work out, Jack," Mom insists. "Don't overreact."

Jack shrugs sarcastically. "Maybe overreacting is exactly what we should be doing," he says. He shoves his chair back under the table and goes down the hall to his room. He doesn't slam his door, but it doesn't latch quietly behind him either.

I look at Mom. She's rubbing her temples with two fingers each.

"Mom?"

Outside, a car passes by, going fast, it sounds like. Someone in the car performs a drive-by cussing, screaming out an open window before disappearing down the block.

"Biiiiiiitch!"

Mom's forehead, already creased, tightens.

"What, Tori."

"Um . . . nothing," I say, and get up. "I'm not very hungry."

Mom doesn't say anything. So I go to my room and close the door.

Maybe I should just plead guilty tomorrow. Maybe that'll make everyone happy.

Kevin Cooper wrote on your timeline.
August 26, two years ago.
Something tells me high school is going to suck, Hershy.

Tori Hershberger Maybe. But maybe not. Do NOT call me Hershy at school!!!

👍Kevin Cooper likes this.

Kevin Cooper Your a jock. Jocks always have more fun. :) And I won't call you that.

👍You like this.

Tori Hershberger Yeah, well, we'll see. ;) How's things with Rachel?

👍Kevin Cooper likes this.

Kevin Cooper Good.

Tori Hershberger Just good?

Kevin Cooper Just good. ;)

👍You like this.

TWO

"It's been six hours since dinner," I tell my friend Noah over the phone, "and I haven't eaten anything since lunch. I'm going to lose all my muscle if this keeps up."

Part of me wants a chicken burrito, and another part is like, *Yeah, right! Good luck keeping that down.*

"You gotta eat, Tori-chan," Noah says. "Jock need food, badly."

I don't answer. I know a bazillion girls who'd kill to have no appetite.

I feel myself wince. That was a poor turn of phrase right now.

"I wish I could sleep," I tell him. "Or do homework, even."

"You're definitely not feeling very good if homework is a reasonable alternative to sleep," Noah says. He's full of it. He gets straight As.

"Hard to do English without a computer," I say.

"True," Noah says. "But you could always use one of those, what do you call them . . . *pencils*?"

I'd probably laugh if tonight wasn't the night that it is. Still, Noah has a point. Maybe I could handwrite some things. Except I don't think my English teacher accepts anything less than twelve-point Times New Roman with one-inch margins. Mom promised to find a laptop from her work that would have an Office suite on it or something, but so far she hasn't. We've all been a *little* preoccupied. But if I don't start turning some things in, there goes junior year.

Speaking of next year . . .

I'm sixteen now, which means if things go badly, I won't get out of prison till I'm twenty-six.

I don't say that to Noah as I sit at my empty desk, holding my phone to my ear and listening to him eat something. Probably popcorn. It's not crunchy enough for chips. I'd hear it if it was chips.

I hate my new phone.

Wait; I should be careful using a word like *hate* right now too. In fact, I'd be happy to never hear it used again.

I should also use quotes around the term "new" phone. It's not *new*-new. Mom had been meaning to recycle it for more than a few years now. It's been sitting on the kitchen counter, in a little clay dish I made in first grade, along with a stew of paper clips, rubber bands, and an outdated Burger King coupon nobody's bothered to throw away. The coupon is so old, it's a family joke. "Hey, buy one, get one free at Burger King!" we'll say whenever someone asks Dad what's for dinner. Mom always sighs and says she knew Canyon City was getting too big when we had *two* Burger Kings instead of one.

Well, at least I've *got* a phone. They didn't completely take away my ability to communicate with the few people who still care to acknowledge me. Which, can I just say, is so hypocritical. As if my teammates didn't give Kevin Cooper a hard time at school. As if the entire coaching staff didn't have it in for him during PE. My God, if ever there was a person who gave Cooper a bunch of crap, it was Coach Scordo, who runs the baseball team and all the boys' PE classes. Any guy who couldn't run a lap got ostracized; I'd seen it. And did administration or the rest of the staff do anything about it? No. Why aren't *they* in trouble too?

Whatever.

I sigh out loud and trace a finger on top of my desk. In addition to switching my phone, my parents also confiscated my laptop, and thus, my lifeline to the wider world. There's still a rectangular dust pattern on my desk from where it used to sit. I should clean that up.

Maybe tomorrow.

"So, Tori-chan?" Noah says on my new/old phone. "You're being awfully quiet. Dare I ask what's on your mind this fine evening?"

"Don't you watch the news?" I ask back. "You know what tomorrow is."

I almost tell him to stop calling me "Tori-chan" instead of just Tori, but right now anything other than Victoria Renée Hershberger is a relief. The TV reporters insist on using all three names, like they do with assassins: Lee Harvey Oswald, John Wilkes Booth. . . .

Hershberger. There is one word to describe this surname: *ghastly*. It looks god-awful beneath last year's freshman Canyon High yearbook photo the news uses all the time. It crowds across my shoulders on my jersey. And it definitely didn't sound any better coming from that stupid reporter during dinner.

"Of course I've been watching," Noah says. "But I don't expect them to tell me the truth."

"I love you," I say.

Noah laughs. "Don't let your mouth write checks your heart can't cash, Hershy."

He's the only person left on planet Earth I'd ever let get away with calling me something like "Hershy." But we go back a long time. Sixth grade. That's virtually an eon. We hung out a lot more back then, in junior high. Even last year. We sort of drifted this year, though. Which makes me all the more grateful that he's sticking by me now.

I lie flat on my bed, staring at the ceiling. "Hey, can you eat a popcorn ceiling?"

"The question is, why would you want to?"

"Because it's popcorn. Duh."

"Pretty sure it's not real popcorn, Tori-chan."

He loves to hear himself say that. Noah wants more than anything to live in Japan. He has this whole spiel about the difference between -*chan* and -*san*. It's cute, but also stale. He's been in love with all things Japanese ever since he first saw *Fullmetal Alchemist*. The obsession grew from there.

"More important, would it taste good with butter and salt?" I say, and answer my own question. "Yes. Everything tastes better with butter and salt. I'd eat my own feet with butter and salt."

"Your own feet, huh?"

"I mean, I'd wash 'em first, obviously."

"That's good, 'cause I've smelled your cleats after a game, and *man. . . .*"

"Shut up."

"Seriously, you guys need to clean up better."

"Says the man crushing on our entire infield."

"Just the infield?" Noah says, feigning shock. "It's the whole team, Hershy."

"I was trying to keep you from sounding like a man whore."

"Yeah, well, man whores get dates," Noah says. "So when's your next game—"

He cuts himself off. I won't be at a game for quite some time. Like, next year, maybe. If I'm lucky. Apparently he forgot.

Or is it *allegedly* he forgot? I can't keep track anymore.

"Well," Noah says after a pause, "I guess, whenever you come back, huh?"

"Yeah," I say. "Sure."

I hear him sigh. "So why'd you call me? To talk about eating your ceiling?"

"Maybe."

"Look, Tori, if you're so totally opposed to talking about it . . ."

"Sorry," I say, very bitchy—bitchily? "Forget it."

I hang up, closing the flip phone. A *flip phone*. A cheap and outdated substitute for my iPhone. May as well be chiseled out of granite. I dump the flip onto my nightstand and fling an arm over my eyes to block out my overhead light. Feels like an interrogation room in here with that blazing corkscrew bulb. "Soft white light," my muscular *ass*.

I didn't mean to be bitchy to Noah, but God, I need a distraction, not more talk about the case. I've been living and breathing nothing else for like a month now. Can't we just talk about dumb things like . . . like popcorn ceilings? Or how hot he thinks Alexis and Alyssa and Taylor and Megan and the rest of the team are?

I wish they'd call me.

Anyway. For all the terrible things about to happen to me, it's kind of a relief to be cranky about my phone or that the light is too bright in here or that my name is so dumb. It's comforting. Reality. Such normal things to be pissy about.

The phone rings, vibrating on the nightstand. *Reeee. Reeee. Reeee.*

I look at my clock. The red digital letters blink from 11:53 to 11:54. A single red dot illuminates the p.m. window. It looks so lonely out there on its own, that little red dot. Doing the same old job, day in, day out. *The time is currently post meridiem,* the little red dot says. *Just so you know.*

Am I getting weirder? Is this what happens when you can't leave the house? Maybe it's cabin fever or Stockholm syndrome or something. Wait, no, that's kidnappers. Whatever.

I pick up the phone and check the teeny-tiny LCD screen. It's Noah on the ID. He's one of the few people whose number I have, and that's only because he called me. If he hadn't, I'd have lost his number forever. It's not like I had it memorized. I didn't have *anyone*'s number memorized. Mom and Dad didn't even take me to the Apple store to try to download my contacts onto the flip before they took my iPhone. They just took it and came back later with this piece of crap.

A contact number transfer probably wouldn't have worked anyway; the technology is too dated on the flip phone. It would've been like teaching Neanderthals to drive a sporty coupe.

"You shouldn't hang up on people like that," Noah says after I open my phone back up.

"Why not?"

"It's rude," he says.

"I've been called worse," I say.

"Don't start that," Noah says.

"Sorry," I say, not bitchily this time. "Can't much help it."

The next words that almost come out of my mouth are, *Noah, I am so scared.* But I don't let them. It won't help.

"So what's your plan tomorrow?" Noah asks, trying very hard to make it a casual question when it is anything but.

My stomach clenches from the inside out, like a series of fists doing a hand-over-hand on my softball bat.

"Try not to pass out, I guess," I say.

"Man, I'm sorry, Tor," Noah says, sympathizing instead of pushing me to divulge my plan for court like those reporters tonight. Like the rest of the world. They can wait a few more hours, all of them.

Noah's willingness to let me not talk specifics is one of the reasons I'm friends with him. He doesn't go straight for the gossip, straight for the big scoop, like the girls on the team would have. Maybe it's better they haven't called, after all.

"I know it's probably a long shot, but is there anything I can do?" Noah asks.

His voice is calm and gentle. I've never kissed Noah, but I would totally make out with his voice if that were possible. His voice and Lucas Mulcahy's arms. Perfect.

I yawn. Finally. I would've gone to bed an hour or two ago except I can't get my mind to stop trampolining. Or, is that a word? Did I just make up a new word? Cool.

"I don't think so," I say to Noah.

"You sure?"

"Yeah," I say. "It's late. I should go to bed."

"Early day at school?" Noah says.

It's a bad joke. Very bad. I don't even have to point it out.

"Sorry," he says right away. "That was stupid. Didn't mean it."

"It's okay," I tell him. "I know. I get it."

"Everyone misses you."

"No, not everyone."

"*I* miss you."

"Thanks," I say, but I'm thinking of Lucas when I say it. Does *he* miss me? The one guy I really want to miss me, I'm not supposed to talk to anymore. I wonder what Lucas is doing tonight? Are those big hands wrapped around a pillow, or folded carelessly beneath his head as he sleeps, confident in his plea tomorrow? What about Marly and the others? Are they already asleep too? I wonder if Lucas is worried. I doubt it. I wonder if he's worried about *me*. I doubt it.

Then I wonder how expensive *his* lawyer is. I'll bet he charges more than Mr. Halpern.

Now I've bummed myself out. Again.

"Noah?"

"Yo."

"What do *you* think I should plead?"

I hear Noah blow out a breath, and imagine him rubbing his eyes with one hand as he says, "Jesus, Tori."

"I'm serious," I say. "I mean, you knew him too. Why don't *you* hate my guts?"

It's so quiet for so long, I imagine I can count each individual drop of rain on my awnings.

"Noah?"

"Look," he says suddenly, "you're right, you should get some sleep. It's probably gonna be a tough day tomorrow, yeah? So just . . . you know, turn off your phone, kill the lights, listen to some music or something . . . just give yourself a break."

"Why aren't you answering the question?"

"I don't—I don't *know* what you should plead, Tori," Noah says. "I know that I don't hate your guts, that I could *never* hate your guts, that I've always—"

He stops. I listen.

"Just shut everything off and forget about it," he says finally. "Okay?"

Not the response I was hoping for. But then again, I'm not entirely sure *what* response I was hoping for.

"Okay," I say. "I'll call you tomorrow when it's over."

Except it won't be over, I think. *It will have just gotten started.*

"Well . . . I dunno, I could stay up or something," Noah says abruptly. "I'm pretty amped on caffeine right now, I can talk if you want. I'll be up anyway. I'm gonna do a chat with some guys in Tokyo. Which probably also means I'll be ditching tomorrow."

"Thanks, but I'm sure," I say. "I'm going to go to sleep. At least, I hope so."

Another pause. He seems to be taking his time answering now. I wonder if I've totally scared him or just made him uncomfortable.

"Okay," Noah says. "Later on. And hey, Tor?"

"Yeah."

"You'll be okay."

Hisssss. A drop of acid burns my eye. At least, that's what it feels like.

"Thanks," I say as salt water pools at the back of my throat.

I end the call before he can say anything else, and toss the phone back to my nightstand.

Thank God for Noah. Despite hearing what the media says about me, he's still around. I'll bet everyone at school only watches the news because they want to see if their particular interview was used or not. Will their *genuine insights into the tragedy* make national news, or just local?

It's probably easy to wish for fame when the spotlight's not on you. Fame sucks.

The flip phone buzzes. I look at the screen, expecting it to be Noah. Who else would it be? Who else *could* it be? I didn't even have Lucas's or Marly's numbers before *or* after my iPhone got taken away. Which honestly makes me mad. Lucas would always give me this look at lunch, like a secret look, you know? Or throw an arm over my shoulders in the hallway sometimes. I thought he was starting to feel the same way about me as I did about him. So what if he put his arm around Marly sometimes too? And Dakota. And some of the cheerleaders.

Whatever. We're not supposed to communicate, anyway. Something tells me *they* are finding a way to do it, though— Lucas and Marly and Dakota and Steve and the other guys. It's just a gut feeling. Maybe because they've known each other longer, or because they're juniors . . . I don't know.

Still staring at the phone screen, I wonder if maybe it's one of my girls, my teammates, finally making contact, ending the big freeze. If I'm found not guilty, will they let me back on the team? Is that what it'll take? Maybe I should ask Coach Hayes. Except she hasn't called either. You wouldn't think a JV softball team in a two-Burger King town could have PR problems of a kind that would make teammates and coaches bounce away like scrimmage balls from a spilled bucket. But I guess it can.

I don't recognize the number at all. It's a local area code but not the same as mine. I shouldn't answer it. It's a crank call. Or worse. "Crank" doesn't really do the term justice. Since I haven't been online in a month, I can only assume someone tracked down my cell number and posted it on Facebook or something, so that everyone on earth can call me and talk trash.

I'm used to it.

I think.

I can't believe my parents went to all the trouble to activate this crappy phone but didn't bother to change the number. Awesome. I need to ask them to correct this.

I flip the phone open, fully expecting a barrage of cuss-words. I spent most of last night writing down a list of fantastic compound, hyphenated swearwords and insults to fire back at the crank callers. I could diagram swearword sentences, sort of like back in eighth grade, when everything was okay and you knew who your friends were.

The red digital numbers blink from 11:59 to 12:00. The single red dot disappears from the p.m. window.

I say, not really caring:

"Hello?"

And no one responds. But I hear something like static. No,

not static. Rain. It's still raining here, too. Harder than during dinner. The patter of it taps on the aluminum awning over my window so fast, it's become monotonous white noise. I think it's similar to what I hear on the other end of the phone—rain tapping and plopping and fading into static.

"If you're going to call me names or something, go ahead," I say to the caller. "Because I've already put your number into Google, and I am more than happy to pay the twenty bucks or so it'll cost me to find out who you are and where you live."

I'm bluffing, of course, as I have neither Google nor money. I probably won't even end up with any of the money Dad put away for school, due to paying Mr. Halpern.

God*dammit* I'm in so much trouble.

"So?" I say. "Go ahead. Just a few more clicks and I'll know everything about you, so you may as well enjoy calling me a bitch or whatever."

Another sound from the other end. A sniffle, I think. A single, stealthy snort. Which is a great name for a children's book. I don't think I'll ever be allowed to write one of those, either. Do publishers do background checks? What about professional softball teams? Will all of this have to go on my college apps?

The caller says, "Why would I call you a bitch?"

It's a guy.

His voice is a flatline, monotone, like the rain. Bit of a rasp to it, like he gargled with 10 percent sandpaper solution, or sings in a hard-core band and had a gig last night.

"I, um . . . I don't. . . . Who is this?"

"Andrew," he says. "Who is *this*?"

"You mean you don't know?" I say.

"No."

"Then why'd you call me?"

Another sniffle. Maybe Andrew has a cold. That's what you get for sitting in the rain.

"It was at random," Andrew says. "I didn't think anyone would actually answer."

He grunts, or maybe laughs, but not in a "Something struck me funny" way. It sort of comes out his nose in a *humph* sound.

"Seriously?" I say, because I can't for one second believe this isn't another crank call.

"The complete randomness of it was the whole point," Andrew says.

I should just hang up, and I know it. But now I'm intrigued. Especially if he really isn't pranking me. Plus, the prankers don't usually take this long. They just call me some name and hang up. Like the car that drove by tonight: *Biiiiiitch!*

Can I just say how unique and clever that one was? It's better than another brick through one of our car windows, though. I guess.

"Ohhh-kay," I say, "why are you calling people at random at midnight on a Thursday, Andrew? Because honestly I was about ready to go to bed."

I don't bother to say, *And stare at my popcorn ceiling for a few hours before getting back up and pacing and lying back down and getting back up and so on,* which is really closer to the truth. Hungry and exhausted, unable to eat or sleep. Woo-hoo.

I *really* need to get some rest for tomorrow. Noah was right. I should've turned the phone off completely.

"Why'd I call you?" he repeats back to me. "Well, that's kind of a long story. Sorry, I'm just . . . still surprised anyone picked up. Wow."

"Right, you expressed your dismay already."

"Not dismay. Shock. Like . . . I dunno, like maybe God's really there after all."

I sit up and dig the fingers of my left hand into my scalp. And yawn.

"Yeah, well, don't get your hopes up," I say. "Now why are you calling me again?"

"Can I ask you something?"

I give him a dramatic sigh. "I guess."

"Do you think God really exists?"

"No," I say. The certainty of it in my voice startles even me.

"How come?"

I take more time answering now. "Because life's not fair."

"Yeah," Andrew says slowly. "I hear ya."

No, you don't, I think. *You have no clue just how bad it can get.* Instead of pointing this out, though, I say, "Now can I ask *you* something?"

"Um. Sure. Why not."

"Why'd you call this number allegedly at random?" There's that word again. *Allegedly.* Maybe if I repeat it enough times, it'll lose its meaning.

I hear the mystery caller take and release a deep breath.

"Honestly?" he says.

"Yeah, honestly."

"Well, honestly . . . because I'm going to kill myself."

Reeee. Reeee. Reeee.

The sound is not my phone buzzing. This time the buzz is in my ears, in my head, a bazillion wasps stinging gray matter.

"You *fucking* dick!" I scream, and slap the phone shut.

So much for my sweet list of compound swearwords. Had to fall back on a classic.

Doesn't make it less true.

Dick. I should've known.

Conversation started October 16, two years ago.

Kevin Cooper did you get our history assignment?

Tori Hershberger Yeah. Where were you today?

Kevin Cooper had to go home

Tori Hershberger Sick?

Kevin Cooper Not exactly. I'm surprised you didn't hear. didnt Jack tell you?

Tori Hershberger Seniors don't talk to FRESHMEN remember? :) Tell me what?

Kevin Cooper big black Magic Marker. my forehead. one word: "pussy."

Tori Hershberger Are you kidding? Who did it?

Kevin Cooper I dont know them. baseball players.

Tori Hershberger Do I know them?

Kevin Cooper doubt it. sophmores or jrs I think.

Tori Hershberger Sorry, Cooper. :(

About the Author

Tom Leveen is also the author of *manicpixiedreamgirl*, *Party*, *Zero* (a YALSA Best Book of 2013), *Sick*, and *Random*. A frequent speaker at schools and conferences, Tom was previously the artistic director and cofounder of an all-ages, nonprofit visual and performing arts venue in Scottsdale, Arizona. He is a native of Arizona, where he lives with his wife and young son.